A
TALE OF
MERMAIDS

A
TALE OF
MERMAIDS

ANN PARKER

The Book Guild Ltd

First published in Great Britain in 2022 by
The Book Guild Ltd
Unit E2 Airfield Business Park,
Harrison Road, Market Harborough,
Leicestershire. LE16 7UL
Tel: 0116 2792299
www.bookguild.co.uk
Email: info@bookguild.co.uk
Twitter: @bookguild

Typeset in 11pt Adobe Garamond Pro

Printed on FSC accredited paper
Printed and bound in Great Britain by 4edge Limited

ISBN 978 1915122 506

British Library Cataloguing in Publication Data.
A catalogue record for this book is available from the British Library.

To everyone who dreams of another life.

ONE

February 1690

Catherine, Alix and Marie-Josèphe were reading in silence when the maid came into the room. Twenty-one, sixteen and twelve years old, the sisters had the same brown hair, round face and blue eyes. They were pretty and lovable with their simple pearl-grey satin dresses.

"Mademoiselle Alix, the master would like to see you in his study."

The girls exchanged a glance. Alix nodded, wondering what she had done to deserve convocation in her father's study. She got up and smoothed her dress before leaving the room. There was almost no light in the corridor, the dark walls and paintings making it gloomy. The only sound she could hear was her feet on the wooden floor. A few minutes after, her heart pounding and her hands shaking, she knocked at the door of the study.

1

"Come in, dear," said Monsieur Lecuyer, his eyes focused on the paper he was reading.

Alix closed the door softly and looked shyly at the room. The fire was weak in the fireplace and her father had to put a blanket on his legs. His study was just like him: cold and austere. Repressing a thrill, Alix stood in the middle of the room, waiting for his goodwill. She pressed her hands together to stop their shaking and forbade herself from looking around. The study was Monsieur Lecuyer's territory and no other member of the household was allowed – not even the maid. Walls covered by books, a simple desk and two chairs were the only furniture. It was basic and useful. A cold light was coming through the windows, just enough to save lighting up the candles. The family was wealthy and there was no need to cut corners, yet Monsieur Lecuyer never allowed any kind of waste.

It seemed to take hours for her father to put down the paper he was reading and look at her. He watched her for a few minutes in awkward silence. This had never happened before. Monsieur Lecuyer spent his life between his study and meetings with other wealthy merchants. Children, especially his daughters, had never been of any interest to him. Alix was surprised and a little bit frightened by this sudden attention. Her father stood up and inspected her from her forehead to her feet before mumbling, "That will do." He then went back to his chair, sat down and started writing. Alix stayed at the centre of the room, motionless as a statue, wondering if he implicitly dismissed her.

After a few minutes, Monsieur Lecuyer raised his head from his papers and smiled formally at his daughter. "Alix, congratulations, you are engaged."

The girl did not have expectations about this talk, but now she was flabbergasted. She tried to remember any mention of a potential alliance for any of the daughters of the house, any unusual friend of their father coming or writing. Nothing. As Alix stayed mute, her father added, "My acquaintance, Count de Kerhoët, is looking for a bride for his nineteen-year-old son, and I thought of you. Catherine is a bit too old for him and Marie-Josèphe too young. You are the perfect match for a quick wedding." Still shocked, Alix could not say a word. Her father added, staring his ice-blue eyes at her, "Aren't you pleased, dear? You will rise above our condition and enter nobility. Count de Kerhoët is from one of the oldest families of Brittany. Their connections and extended family will also help me hold an administrative position and a title of nobility."

Alix vividly imagined her father rubbing his hands together in contentment. "Yes, Father. This is wonderful news," she managed to mutter.

Obviously really pleased with himself and his achievement, Monsieur Lecuyer did not notice the lack of happiness or excitement in his daughter's voice. And, to be honest, he would not have cared. His own marriage was a financial arrangement and he intended for his children to help him enrich his fortune, connections and social position. "Good. I am pleased."

Fighting to retain her tears, Alix asked with a trembling voice, "When will the wedding be?"

"On your eighteenth birthday, so in almost two years."

Alix felt relieved: at least she would have the time to get used to it. Immune to his daughter's feelings and concerns,

Monsieur Lecuyer added, "But you are going to live with them from next summer, to become familiar with the family and the correct behaviour of a countess. You won't be a merchant's daughter anymore!"

Alix was not moving, not thinking and not crying. She was almost not breathing. She was just standing in the middle of the room, her face paler than usual, too shocked to have any reaction. Losing any interest in his daughter, Monsieur Lecuyer went back to his desk and started writing a note. "That's all, Alix, you can leave now."

"Yes, Father. Thank you, Father," she muttered before closing the door.

She went back to the living room, her sisters reading in silence on their sofas.

"What did Father want?" asked Catherine, her eyes not moving from the page she was reading.

"I am engaged and I will leave home next summer."

Catherine turned her page. "Great, congratulations, Alix... You will be missed," she added after few seconds.

Marie-Josèphe barely reacted, mumbling some congratulations. Alix always knew she was not close to her sisters – or her brothers, for that matter – but she would have never thought that the prospect of her leaving and, perhaps, never returning to Paris would be met with so much indifference. Holding back her tears, Alix sat back at her place and opened her book, finding the silence more oppressive than before.

July 1690

Travelling was long and harassing. The carriage was far from comfortable and it was incredibly warm with the summer heat. Alix had been crying intermittently for about three weeks. Now, locked in the stuffed carriage, warm and alone, she had time to think about her new life: would her husband be nice? Good-looking? What about her in-laws? Would they accept her? She was wondering if they would be as cold as her own family. As a child, she had often speculated about other families: were they the same, or did they enjoy spending time together?

The Lecuyer house was divided with the male area on one side and on the other, the female one. Even as a child, except at dinner, Alix would not see her father and brothers. It took her many years to realise that they were actually living under the same roof. What they did during the days was a complete mystery to her; she did not even know what sort of trade her family was involved in. She had to spend her time with her odd and dispassionate sisters, first acquiring an education, then sewing or reading in silence. She could not even remember playing with them. The family was very wealthy, so they all had their set of rooms and did not meet with the others unless it was necessary. Alix's childhood memories were full of alone time and self-sufficiency.

That day, she was so dehydrated that she could not cry anymore. It was barely the early afternoon and she had already drunk all the water she had; and no stop would be made until the evening. Her new family asked her not to bring anyone, so she was travelling alone, under the surveillance of two her father's manservants. Anyone else would feel lonely, but it was actually quite close to the life she was used to: there could be ten people in a room, yet it was always silent, everyone focusing on a book or a sewing work. She had books to read, and despite the warmth, she was wishing for the travel not to end. "Better the devil you know," says the proverb, and for Alix it worked perfectly with her family.

The following morning, Joseph, one of the manservants, told her that they would arrive in the afternoon at Beg Hastel. Isolated from everyone and everything, Alix did not know what to expect. Would it be a mansion? Would it be a castle? Would it be one of those strange-looking houses with a thatched roof? And the scarier questions: what was her new family like? Would her fiancé like her? Would they be like her family? She felt her level of anxiousness increasing at every mile. She could not eat or even drink during the day, her stomach twisting with apprehension. That morning, she did not dare look at her own reflection: all her dresses wrinkled by the journey, her hair untidy and no proper bath for weeks. She felt dirty and was well aware that she stank.

When the carriage stopped, Alix was about to faint. Holding Joseph's hand, she went out and was dazzled by the July sun. She felt on another world: the fresh and salty air, the sky so blue she confounded it with the sea, the seagulls and the massive and dark silhouette of the castle – everything was completely different from Paris. It was not a mansion but an old and stately castle with four round towers on the side, a dungeon in the middle and a moat on two sides. Alix was breathless. It was the most imposing construction she had seen in her entire life, even more massive than Notre Dame.

She was so hypnotised by the view that she did not realise that people were around her.

"Alix, I presume," asked a lady. The girl turned her head in that direction, her face haggard. The lady was around forty years old, slim with a beautiful face.

"Yes, it's me." She felt like an idiot; her brain was empty and tears on the edge of her eyelid. She did not even realise that she did not curtsey.

"Oh dear, I am so glad that you arrived safe and sound! We are so happy to welcome you in our family! I am Louise de Kerhoët," said the Countess before hugging Alix. The girl was shocked. Except maybe her nanny a couple of times many years ago, nobody ever hugged her or even touched her. The tears started to burn, but she tried to keep them at bay. And smile. Smiling was the great trick taught to girls to put up a front for the world, to give the impression that an arranged marriage was not bad news or the absence of dear ones not a fatality. So she smiled and kept her tears for when she would be alone.

"And I am delighted to join your family."

"Well, well, well. Let me introduce you to the rest of us." She indicated a handsome boy and a pretty girl, roughly the same age as Alix. "Here is my son Louis, your fiancé, and his sister Marguerite." Alix wanted to do a curtsey, but the girl took her hands and had a warm smile.

"I am so happy to finally have a sister!" She sounded very enthusiastic, whilst her brother just looked at the new girl with curiosity.

The Countess looked up to heaven before gently scolding her daughter. "Marguerite, please, restrain yourself! The poor girl just arrived and needs to rest! My dear Alix, come with me, I will show you your room and you will have proper time to rest and take care of yourself. I haven't done the journey to Paris for a long time, but I recall how horrific it was. You must be exhausted!"

The Countess took Alix's arm and made her way to the castle. The girl was just able to have a quick glance at her fiancé. A tall, young, blond count. The sun was making his blond hair shine like gold; she could not see his face fully, but she thought he was very handsome.

The castle was nicely refreshing after the outside warmth. Windows were high and small, creating a very dark atmosphere, which was reinforced by the austere look of the dark grey stones and the minimalist decoration. No painting on the walls, no flowers, no thick carpets on the floor to warm the interior. In just a few minutes, Alix started feeling cold; by the time she reached her room, she was freezing. During the journey to her room, the Countess was lively – chatting, not really waiting for an answer. When they arrived at the bedroom, Alix was almost crying. The kindness of the Countess, her obvious desire to make her future daughter-in-law comfortable, actually made her uneasy. Unused to such behaviour and exhausted by the travel, the girl did not know how to react. She was doing her best to retain her tears, nodding her head from time to time and muttering small encouragements.

"You are welcome to go anywhere in the castle except the North Tower – it is old and in need of repairs, so please do not go and risk being injured." Alix was too tired to properly answer. She just nodded when the Countess turned towards her. "Here is your bedroom," she added, with an excited voice while she was letting the girl go in. Alix was not able to see anything. The Countess realised it and added, in a compassionate voice, "You must be very tired after that dreadful journey, my dear girl. I will let you rest and we will talk later, alright?"

Alix was grateful for that kindness and tact. She smiled faintly and whispered a thank-you. The Countess left her after a last worried glance, and the girl threw herself on the comfortable bed before falling into a dreamless sleep.

She awoke hours later. She could not say how long she had slept, but the sun was lowering in the sky. The castle was quiet and peaceful. No sign of anyone else. Alix decided to have a proper look at her new bedroom. As in the rest of the castle, the walls were made of a dark stone. The canopy bed was the main piece of furniture in the room: double, fitted with the finest linen sheets and an exquisitely embroidered dark blue bedspread. The thick velvet curtains of the bed were of the same shade of blue. For the rest of the room, a couple of chests and a dressing table completed the furniture. Her luggage had been brought into the room while she was napping. She slept so heavily that she did not realise it. She went to the dressing table, poured a drop of water into a cup and, with a cloth, washed her face, neck and chest. The cold liquid was a delight on her skin. Alix would have liked a bath or at least a more careful toilet, but she was afraid to be perceived as rude if she did not join her hosts.

"Your *family*. Your new family," she corrected herself out loud. It seemed odd, almost immoral to say so, to think so. But what was her real family, she wondered. A cold house in Paris, filled with icy people. None of them would miss her and she would probably not miss them either. Strangely, it was not even making her feel sad: she had a new family, a fresh start, a chance to have a bit of happiness. She decided that she would not ruin that. She sat in front of the mirror and rearranged her hair. As she was not used to doing so, it took her a bit of time. She finally left the room when she was satisfied with her appearance.

The corridor was already dark, slightly illuminated by a few candles. She did not know where to go: right or left? Alix vaguely remembered coming from the left-hand side, so she decided to go back there, hoping to find someone who could send her in the right direction. Even though the corridor was dark and cold, it did not feel as empty as her house in Paris. Alix smiled, uncertain of the destination but convinced she would enjoy the journey. Thinking back, she might have been overdramatic in crying all the way from Paris; it looked like she had traded a wealthy but emotionally poor family with a very welcoming, friendly new family. She was so lost in her thoughts that she did not see Marguerite arriving.

"Alix! I am so happy to see you awake. I was coming to your room to see if you needed anything, but it is so much better to find you up. You can join us for dinner now."

Alix was startled by the appearance of her almost sister-in-law and even more surprised by her friendliness. She observed her: Marguerite's blonde hair appeared as liquid gold with the light of the candles. She was a bit smaller than Alix with a slender body and fair skin. Her face was a bit long but harmonious with a small mouth and candid brown eyes. Alix was not used to so much friendliness and she was not sure how to react. Should she be just as friendly? She did not know how to, so it would sound fake. Be cold? It would sound like an insult. Marguerite did not let her dither any longer. She took her arm and started to walk towards the dining room, Alix graciously accompanying.

"Dear, dear Alix, you truly are one of a kind! There is no need to be shy, we are family!" Marguerite cheerfully said. "Soon we will be sisters and we will do so much together. Actually, let's not wait to become sisters to spend time together. The weather is absolutely lovely this summer. We must go on a sightseeing trip. The cliffs are absolutely beautiful! Have you ever seen one?"

After weeks locked in a carriage and a lifetime of quiet whispering as the only type of communication, Alix was surprised by such animated – and almost loud – chatter. Marguerite was everything she had been taught was unladylike and did everything she had been taught not to do. Yet, she found her endearing and knew she must answer if she wanted to fit in the family.

She cleared her throat. "No, I have never seen a cliff before. I actually have never been outside of Paris before coming here."

Even more excited to receive an answer, Marguerite kept on going with her babble. "Cliffs are nothing compared to Paris! I have heard so much about the city, that it is beautiful and full of life. That the women there are the most beautiful in the world, and so are the men, and so courteous. Have you ever been to the theatre? To a ball?" Marguerite stopped walking and intensely looked at Alix. She then smiled. "You are so pretty, you must have had so many suitors fighting for your attention!"

Marguerite looked at Alix expectantly; the young woman was not sure how to answer. She had never done any of that… She remembered her family home, big but so narrow, cold and dark. Through the window, she could see other houses as dark and narrow; people on the streets looking busy and grim, some better dressed than the others, but nothing special. Once a week, with her sisters, she was allowed on a walk to a nearby park – under the surveillance of their maid and a manservant. They were not allowed to talk to anyone. No one tried to talk to them anyway…

She blushed and answered, stammering a little, "Well, my father is quite strict, so we were not allowed to go to the theatre or outside of the house, really." Her father was really adamant that theatres were sinful places and that only unvirtuous women went there.

Surprised, Marguerite looked at Alix. "What did you do all day long?"

"Well, we read, sew and prayed a lot."

"What do you mean, you prayed a lot?"

"We are Jansenists. We believe that only a certain portion of humanity is predestined to be saved, therefore, only perfect contrition can save us. Jansenists do their best to not sin, but we also pray a lot to ensure that our souls will be saved." Alix was becoming confident and passionate as she spoke. "My aunt Louise joined the abbey of Port-Royal-des-Champs when she was young and, even though it is forbidden now, my older sister, Agnès, joined her a few years ago."

Her declaration was met by silence and some sort of confusion from Marguerite, who had never heard about Jansenism or Port-Royal-des-Champs. She shrugged, not

12

interested in discovering more about the topic. "Here we are Catholics and we go to Mass every Sunday."

Alix opened her mouth to specify that Jansenism was also Catholic, but she realised it would lead to a long and disheartening discussion, so she decided not to say any more, as she was still tired by her travel and did not want to be labelled as a bore on her first day in her new family. She still asked, "What will we do the rest of the time if we only go to Mass on Sunday?"

"We will be naughty!" said Marguerite with a wicked smile before resuming her walking.

"Won't it be hard then to access perfect contrition?"

Marguerite started to laugh. "Who says I want to do that?"

Startled and afraid for her new sister, it was Alix's turn to stop in the corridor. "Don't you want your soul to be saved and to access Heaven?"

Marguerite shrugged. "Don't you believe that not everyone goes there?"

Alix nodded. "Yes, but I also believe that with some effort, we can do it and have a peaceful eternal afterlife."

Marguerite cast a strange look that Alix could not decipher. It made her remember her father when he had looked at her in his office in February, assessing her. She shivered and, when Marguerite smiled, she forgot about the strange feeling.

"Then I promise you we will not be too naughty. Actually, we will spend our days together, so you can assess what I do wrong."

Overjoyed by the conversation and the good nature of her new sister, Alix hugged her. It had never happened before and she felt very embarrassed until Marguerite wrapped her arms around her and returned the hug, laughing. Smiling, they took each other's arm and went to the dining room.

The room was long and clearly built for holding a party. Two chimneys on each side, giant candelabras hanging from the ceiling, delicate sculptures decorating the walls. This room showed the grandeur, power and fortune of the family. If only a small table was prepared in the room, its ornaments were refined: silver cutlery, plates of the most exquisite porcelain and crystal glasses. The whole family – Louise and Louis – was gathered around a fire, obviously waiting for Marguerite. Hearing the sound of their footsteps, Louise turned an annoyed face towards the two girls, but her scowl was replaced by a warm smile when she saw Alix. She came to her, her arms outstretched and her palms open; she took the girl's hands in hers, ignoring Marguerite.

"Dear Alix, what a wonderful surprise! I had hope you would feel better, but you seem perfectly rested. I am delighted that you are able to join us for dinner. Louis, come greet your fiancée, isn't she beautiful?"

Following his mother's command, Louis came and examined a blushing Alix. From the piercing look of his eyes to the sly smile on his lips, she felt deeply uncomfortable.

Like a mirage, his expression transformed to one of sheer admiration and he bowed to peck her right cheek. "Absolutely wonderful indeed, Mother. With such a charming fiancée, all the men in the area will be jealous of my luck!"

Still uncomfortable – both because of her fiancé and his gallant attitude, and the openness and warmth of her mother-in-law – Alix just smiled, feeling her cheeks burning.

Noticing the awkwardness of the girl, Louise commented, "We are embarrassing you, aren't we? Children, let's take place at the table and help this poor lamb feel at home."

Louis offered Alix his arm to walk the short distance to the table, pulled her chair to allow her to sit. She did her best to diminish her awkwardness, pretending that she was used to such gestures. She was not sure if she had fooled Louise and Louis, but when she looked at Marguerite sitting in front of her, she could see that her new friend was biting her lip so as not to laugh. Alix felt both a surge of embarrassment and a smile creeping on her lips. She looked away, focusing her attention on the servants bringing out food. She also noticed the odd setting of the table: it was a large rectangle with Louise on one short side, an empty seat in front of her; on one long side, Alix seated on Louise's right and Louis' left with empty seats in front of her and on his right. Marguerite was in front of Louis, also surrounded by two empty seats. Frowning, she tried to understand the meaning of such a strange table plan.

"These are the seats of my husband and younger son." Louise's voice startled Alix. "They are away on a business trip—"

Marguerite snorted; Louise turned to her and coldly scolded her, "Marguerite, please show some decorum; you are not a lowly servant!"

The girl bowed her head, not quick enough to hide the anger in her eyes. Louise turned to Alix, who was observing the scene, trying to understand the dynamic between the two women; Louis had quietly started to eat, not paying attention to the quarrel.

"Dear Alix, my apologies. Marguerite tends to be a bit wild and forgets her manners…" She cut a small piece of meat and shot a warning glance at Marguerite. "As I was saying, my husband and younger son are away on a business trip, which unfortunately happens often… You see, Louis will inherit our family estate and fortune, so my husband decided to ensure that our younger son, Henri, will be able to earn his own money."

"That is very laudable of your husband, but isn't it more common to enter the army?" asked Alix. It was her understanding that a noble family would give their second son to the army and the third one to the clergy. Her own family being merchants, it was just normal for her brothers to learn the trade. In any case, children did not have a choice.

"Indeed, you are very observant, my dear child. We thought of doing that, of course, but Henri does not have the soul of a soldier and it broke my heart to force him to become something he hated." From the corner of her eye, Alix saw Marguerite making a face, but Louise kept talking so she focused her interest back on her. "My husband, being a kind man, agreed for Henri to learn business, and he decided to follow him to ensure his safety."

"This is very commendable of both you and your husband; so many parents would care only about tradition and reputation instead of the happiness of their own children."

Alix stopped talking, smiling before eating another bite. Yet she was not hungry anymore, realising that it was what had happened to her: her father had sold her for a position and a chance to join the aristocracy. She smiled. *A position to try to join the aristocracy; he will never go higher than being a noble of robe, the lowliest kind of nobility.* She resumed eating her food, still not hungry, but her instinct told her to show no weakness.

The evening was very pleasant: after dinner, they went to a living room where Marguerite offered – to her mother and brother's great surprise – to read the Bible. She had a lovely voice and read quite well despite stumbling on some words – Alix wondered what kind of education she had received to seem so unfamiliar with the Bible and read so poorly. She immediately chastised herself for thinking badly of her new sister, her new friend. Louise then played the harp, an instrument that Alix had never heard and was delighted to see in action. Her fingers were running on the strings quickly and confidently, the melody was pure and Louise's voice delightfully harmonious. All in all, it was the best evening the girl had had in a while – to be truthful, the best evening she had ever had. When came the time for everyone to get back in their rooms, Louise called on servants and brought a young woman, barely older than Alix, with big brown eyes and an easy smile.

"Dear Alix, this is Thérèse; she will be your maid from now on. Girl, bring Lady Alix to her room."

"Yes, Your Ladyship," said Thérèse whilst bowing down.

"Dear Alix, I wish you good night and will see you at breakfast tomorrow. I also remind you not to venture to the North Tower; it is too dangerous."

Louise turned around and left through a door, followed by Louis and Marguerite, who made a small hand gesture towards Alix. Feeling dismissed, the young woman turned to Thérèse and they started to walk through the dark corridors back to her room. After turning around several times, Alix started to laugh.

"I do not know if I will ever find my way in the castle."

"Of course you will, My Lady," answered Thérèse immediately. "I arrived just a few weeks ago and now I know all the ways by heart."

"Oh, where do you come from?" asked Alix, ashamed to have assumed that the maid had been here for a long time.

Thérèse shrugged. "A small village, on the lands owned by the Count. They were looking for a maid for your arrival and I wanted to escape an arranged marriage, so everything was for the best."

Even though she was glad that Thérèse had managed to escape an unwanted marriage and its obvious unhappiness, Alix was suddenly feeling that she was in a similar situation, though with no escape. She did not know Louis and one evening was far from enough to ensure that they would get along – especially as he did not speak much to her, or anyone. Not realising her new mistress' distress, Thérèse kept on chatting about the castle, how kind the Countess was, how excited she was to become a personal maid. Strangely, Alix was thankful for this soliloquy that made her feel less lonely. Every time that Thérèse was looking at her, she managed to bring a smile on her face, and soon the dark thoughts went back to hide in a small corner of her brain. *Before deciding that this marriage will be unhappy, I must get to know Louis and discover his personality*, she decided. Feeling relieved and at ease with the future, she reached her room and was helped by Thérèse into her night gown. The maid closed the curtains and revived the fire.

"I will wake you up at 8am to be ready for breakfast at 8.30," announced Thérèse.

"I would like to have a bath before if it is possible, I did not have an opportunity to wash properly for some time and I would feel much better if I could bathe…" said Alix, feeling the need to justify her request.

Thérèse nodded. "I will request it from the kitchen right now and will wake you up a bit earlier so you can have the time to enjoy the water."

Alix smiled. "That will be perfect."

"Good night, My Lady," said the maid, curtseying.

"Thank you and good night, Thérèse," responded Alix.

Listening to the faltering footsteps, Alix smiled, feeling more confident about her future at Beg Hastel with the Kerhoëts. She went to bed and, despite her long nap earlier, fell asleep within minutes.

TWO

The great pirate Vivien Harlock was born on August 6, 1672, daughter of Steve Harlock and Mary Kane. She had three older siblings (Garrett, Patrick and Judith) and two younger twin sisters (Elizabeth and Ann) – she did not know about the stillborn babies and the miscarriages. Her parents had come from England in the hope of having a decent life in the colonies. It ended up being wishful thinking and the family lived in extreme poverty. Settled in Delaware, near Georgetown, the Harlocks had big lands but not enough arms to cultivate them. Respectively aged ten and nine, Garrett and Patrick were already in the fields, doing what they could for their parents, but they were neither old nor strong enough to make a real difference. Mary Kane was doing everything she could to help her husband, leaving Judith to take care of the rest. At only seven years old, Judith was able to prepare bread, soup and porridge; she took care of the house, the cow and chickens, and, most importantly, her younger siblings. More than their mother, she loved and raised her three sisters and taught them everything she knew.

Even at a very young age, Vivien struggled to find her place in this life. She was neither a homemaker nor a farmer, but she found her own way to help her family by wandering into the woods with a basket to collect wild fruits and mushrooms. Her parents even agreed to her request of planting the pits of the fruits in a part of their land in the hope of having their own orchard. When she was about eight, a couple of Indians came to make some trade with the farmers of Georgetown. Vivien went with her father (or rather followed him, as he forbade her to leave the farm) and was absolutely enchanted by the vision of those men with their tribal paintings, their odd clothing and their bows. That day, in the small marketplace of a tiny town, Vivien fell in love with archery and Michael Tanner, the son of another farmer. He was a few years older than her and he looked like an angel with honey hair and eyes green as the grass in spring. After that day, Vivien built her own bow and used it to hunt – that new skill was most welcomed by her family, who finally could eat meat regularly. They also tanned the skins and used them to make bedcovers and winter clothes. Vivien purposely hunted around the Tanner's farm, hoping to catch a glimpse of Michael – often without any luck: even though the youngest son of John Tanner, Michael, had many chores that required him to work in the field or in the barn.

August 1682

About two years after the day in the marketplace, Vivien's luck turned. She was hunting when she heard some noises coming from a small lake. Out of curiosity, she went around and hid in the bushes to see what was happening. She started to smile when she recognised Michael Tanner with his three older brothers playing in the water. She enjoyed the view for a bit, until she grasped that they were likely to be naked. Feeling uneasy about that, she decided to leave, but in her haste (and slight embarrassment), she was not as careful as usual and did not realise that the oldest brother – a sixteen-year-old named John Junior (JJ) – had noticed her and sneaked up on her. He took her by the waist and brought her closer to the lake.

"Brothers, look what I found in the bushes. That little girl was spying on us."

Vivien, who had stayed motionless when he took her, found both her mobility and voice back. "Absolutely not! I was just hunting!"

JJ and his brothers laughed. "Hunting? You are just a little girl playing with," he critically examined her weapons, "a badly made bow. You won't hurt many prey with that."

Absolutely furious, Vivien kicked him in the thigh. With a cry of pain, he let her go for a second then tried to reach for her, but she bit his hand and gave him another kick in the knee before running through the forest like a wild animal. His brothers were frozen in the water, too surprised by the vivacity and the aggressiveness of the girl to interfere. She ran aimlessly and found shelter under an old tree whose roots were over ground. Her heart was beating fast and her breath was rapid. She replayed the scene in her head. *What did I do? Why did I have to do that?* Her parents had always said she was impulsive and she had always dismissed them, but now she must agree with them. In just a few minutes, she had ruined her chances to make a good impression on Michael and all the Tanner family. *I hope they didn't recognise me. Mother and Father would die of shame if they knew what I had done.* She went back home that night empty-handed and her head down; Judith noticed that something was wrong but Vivien was mortified and refused to tell her what had happened.

The following days, she went back to hunt but avoided the lands around the Tanner farm; she also wore two knives in case the boy came to have his revenge. She saw some broken branches and followed the path silently, hoping for a deer. And she was right. It was in a clearing, eating grass peacefully. Vivien took a moment to admire the animal before bending her bow. *One, two...* Before she could fire, a branch had cracked, allowing the deer to sense the danger and escape. With her bow still bent, Vivien turned towards the noise and saw Michael. She frowned and he put his hands up.

"I am sorry," he started nervously. "I did not want to scare your prey."

"What do you want?" asked Vivien without amenity. She was concentrating very hard on not being nice; he was even handsomer than she remembered.

"Nothing. Well, not really, I was looking for you, I—"

She cut in. "Are you here to take revenge for your brother?"

Michael looked at her, his green eyes showing surprise. He then laughed. "Certainly not – that was the best thing ever!"

Still frowning, Vivien lowered her bow. "How so?"

"JJ is the oldest, and as he will inherit the farm, he always bosses us around and we absolutely hate it. After seeing him

23

beaten by a little girl, Matt and Joe did not stop laughing for days!"

Vivien was annoyed at him calling her a 'little girl'. She was ten, after all, not a baby like Elizabeth or Ann. She bit her cheek so she would not tell him off.

"So I don't have to fear retaliation from your family?"

He shook his head, still amused. "No, and JJ was so ashamed and annoyed that he did not mention the incident to our parents. However," at that point he became very serious, "if you see him around, don't stay. You hurt his pride a great deal and I don't think he will forgive you anytime soon."

Vivien nodded and turned to leave when Michael stepped forward. "Wait! That's not why I followed you."

Still wary, Vivien kept her hands on the bow and arrow before turning towards the boy. He made another step forward and she tensed a bit, but she could see that he had no weapons. Now, he was close enough for her to see the freckles on his nose and cheeks.

"Why then?"

He enthusiastically indicated her weapons. "Your bow. I want to make one and learn how to use it; I want to be like the Indians who came to town years ago!"

Vivien stayed silent, stunned that the boy had had the same feelings as her. Maybe they were not so different after all. *We will spend time together, getting to know each other, and maybe he will love me too.* She blushed at her thoughts.

Michael interpreted her silence as a refusal, lowering his head in disappointment. "I will let you go back to your hunt then – have a good day."

Stricken by the sudden change of tone, Vivien looked at Michael quickly walking away. She understood that she had missed a good opportunity, probably the only one to get to know him. Panicking a bit, she shouted, "Wait!"

She ran after him. He turned towards her, hope shining in his eyes.

"I will show you, if you still want," Vivien added timidly.

The bright and unequivocally happy smile that appeared on Michael's face answered her.

Over the next months, they became close, going almost every day in the forest to track animals. Vivien showed the boy how to make his own bow and arrows, how to hunt, and where she had found the best places to hunt. Even though being wealthier than the Harlocks, the Tanners appreciated the extra meat Michael now brought home. The two families knew each other from Sunday's church services but never particularly hit off as the Harlocks had poor social standing in the community. The friendship between their children changed that and – fairly reluctantly – both families were forced to socialise. As much as Vivien was happy to get closer to Michael's family, the downside was that JJ had recognised her and she could see hatred in his eyes. He now knew her name and where she lived; he was too smart to attack her frontally, and she was sure that, one day, he would sneak up on her. Vivien was afraid, but she decided that she would not show her fear to him or anyone else. No one would know and try to protect her; she would do that all by herself. From then on, the little girl had several knives hidden in her clothing, ready for the day JJ would strike.

June 1686

Years passed and it seemed like JJ had forgotten about her. He was sixteen when the incident had occurred and soon became more interested in girls of his own age than in Vivien – she hoped that the fact that neither his brothers nor she ever mentioned the incident to anyone made him at ease that no one knew about his shameful secret. Yet Vivien did not let her guard down, always wearing weapons and always being careful of her surroundings. The anticipation of retaliations that never happened made her a bit paranoid. She often wondered if it would not have been better to go to him and let him beat her once and for all instead of living with constant unease.

Even though she was fourteen, Vivien refused to leave her hunting days behind to become a homemaker. She refused to stay home all day cooking and cleaning like her sisters; in winter, feeding the cow and the chickens, and tanning the skins, were their only outings. In a way, Vivien refused to grow up; she wanted to remain a free child, doing her best to ignore the changes of her body and the attitudes of adults around her. Her unique position as provider of fresh meat made it so that even though her mother wanted her to stay in the house, her father thought that having her out, hunting, was a much-needed complement to their ordinary lives. They were also selling the skins in the town market, which allowed them to add birds in the pen.

One hot summer afternoon, Michael and Vivien were hanging out on a pond: they had built a raft and were excited to use it any time they wanted. Michael turned to Vivien and admired her for a minute before speaking: she had heavy brown hair, matte skin darkened by the sun; her eyes were closed but he knew they were grey and unfathomable – after years of being her friend, he still did not know what she thought. She had a small but harmonious frame; he was sure that within a few years, she would be a beauty. He had something to say and he was not sure how she would react.

"Vi?"

"Mmmm?"

"I need to talk to you."

Her heart missed a beat. She knew the day was coming: Michael had been so different the past few weeks, distracted, daydreaming on their hunts and distant. The only reason she could think of was that he liked a girl, but she could not imagine where he would have met her, as they spent their days together and he was with his family the rest of the time. She quietened her flimsy heart and opened her eyes.

"I'm listening."

"I'm leaving for Georgetown."

Vivien's relief was brief, and she changed position to face him. "Why? Why would you go there? Our lives are here!"

Michael stayed silent for some time and her fears came back. *Maybe he met a girl from there and decided to follow her...* Neither his face darkening with embarrassment nor his long silence helped her feel better, his eyes lost in the scenery.

Finally, he decided to talk with an uncertain voice. "I am my parents' last son; I have no right to inherit anything and they are not wealthy enough to provide lands or anything for me. I must create my own future, find my path, so I have decided to enrol on a merchant marine vessel."

Without saying anything, Vivien sat on the raft, her back towards the boy, to hide her tears. In the stretching silence, she let go of her pain, crying as silently as possible. *It would have been less painful if he had told me he was getting married – at least I would have been able to see him sometimes.* She was so lost in her thoughts that she did not hear Michael moving towards her. He then caressed her wild hair, which gave her shivers.

"Vi?"

She turned her tear-soaked face towards Michael. He let go of her hair and put his hands on each side of her face, drying her skin with his callous thumbs. He had a strange expression on his face; she had seen it before, a brief and intense gaze that came more often lately, yet she never understood it. Normally, he would go back to his usual facial expression, but that day he did not and, perplexed, she frowned.

He took a big breath. "I wanted to ask you…" Suddenly, he blushed and started to remove his hands from her face, but Vivien put her hands on top of his.

"What?" she asked softly.

He intensely looked at her again and blurted out, "Would you wait for me?"

To say that Vivien was surprised was an understatement; she had never thought that Michael was feeling the same as her and now that he had expressed an interest, she was mute. And she blushed. Vivien was furious with herself for being so predictable. The blush was, however, a good sign for Michael, who interpreted it as proof that the young girl had feelings for him too.

After a last caress of her cheeks, he took her hands in his.

"I know that I won't inherit anything, but I hope to make a good life for myself in the merchant marines. I will go away for a few years until I have enough money for us to start our life; and when I'm back, I will ask your father for your hand."

He finished his sentence, breathless and hopeful. Vivien could see it in his eyes, with a tinge of fear. *Does he think I will reject him?* She shook her head to push away the stupid thought. However, the boy misinterpreted her gesture and let her hands go. Seeing the hurt and disappointment in his eyes, Vivien hastily answered in a voice a bit too loud, "Yes! I will wait for you and marry you."

Relief and utter contentment washed over Michael. He had never known what being happy meant until that moment. He looked at his friend, now lover, the most confident, fierce and strong girl he had never met, and smiled as if she was offering him the most wonderful gift. Vivien smiled too and, for once, he was able to read her grey eyes, and all he could see was love. He came closer and kissed her; it was sweet, slow and inexperienced. Perfect for them. They broke the kiss and looked at each other, smiling. *This is the happiest moment of my life; until we are married, nothing will top it,* she thought whilst Michael brought her body closer to his. His arm was around her shoulders and her head on his chest, where she could hear his steadily beating heart. They stayed immobile under the sun, in their bubble, for long minutes until the prospect of Michael's departure came back to Vivien's mind.

"When are you leaving?" she asked in a small voice.

She felt Michael tensing and he let the silence stretch. She moved away from him, feeling immediately cold despite the warm temperature. "So?"

Michael looked guilty and lowered his glance. "Tomorrow, at dawn," he answered timidly.

Vivien was shocked. How long had he been planning to leave? How long had it been since he had decided the date? She had been living on borrowed time without knowing it and she felt betrayed. She remembers JJ's cocky smile the previous Sunday at church, and she realised that he had known. And worse, he had known that she did not. Rage came through her and she had to force herself to stay immobile. Michael looked up and realised that he had never seen Vivien that worked up by something since the time she had beaten up JJ. Her whole body was tensed and he could see she was simmering with anger – all of that because of him.

"I am so sorry, Vi. I could not bring myself to tell you before. It was selfish of me not to want to see you sad." He could see her receding fury and some tears in her eyes. He put his right hand on her cheek and she leaned into it. He came closer and put his left hand on her waist. "I was also afraid that you would not share my feelings, so I wanted to have as many good memories of you as I could. I am sorry I was not braver."

The last words were murmured whilst he put his forehead on hers. Vivien's anger disappeared and she felt both the happiness of loving and being loved, and the sadness of knowing an adored one is leaving.

She caressed his cheek in return and answered with a sly smile, "If you had talked to me before, we would have had more time to kiss."

Once more, Michael gave her his bright and warm smile, and, despite everything, Vivien felt she was the luckiest girl in the kingdom. They kissed again, and again, and again – until the sun started to set and the wind became cold. They both had passed dinnertime, but they could not let go of each other. Michael accompanied Vivien to her family's farm, holding her hand. Each step made them sadder and quieter, but their grip on each other's hand was becoming stronger, to the point of being painful.

"I want to see you tomorrow before you leave," asserted Vivien.

Michael hugged her, kissing her forehead. "No, my love, it will make everything harder if you see me."

"But—"

"Please, Vi, I don't know if I will be able to leave if you are there."

"Then don't!"

Michael hugged her. "I must, you know that. It's for us, for our future."

In his arms, Vivien stayed silent. She wanted to scream that it was not for them; it was solely for him. To quench his thirst for adventure and money. They could make it if they stayed here, she knew it. Yet, she loved him and did not say anything, silently shedding a few more tears, enjoying his warm embrace. After some long minutes, they finally broke their embrace. Michael gave Vivien one last kiss and stepped back.

"I will write to you as often as I can."

She nodded, not having the heart to tell him that she could not read. If it ever came to that, she would find someone to help her with it. The pastor, maybe.

"Good night, Vi."

"Good night, Mike."

They parted and she did her best to keep the tears at bay. Once she entered the house, her parents went to her, asking questions, not waiting for her answers and deciding that she would go to sleep without dinner. Vivien did not mind: she was not hungry; she just wanted to sleep and forget for a while that her lover was going away…

January 1688

The days after Michael's departure had turned into weeks and months – eighteen, to be precise. Vivien had only received three letters during that time, all mentioning how much Michael missed her but how enjoyable working on a ship was. It was demanding and tiring (he had also had to change ship as the captain of the first was abusive towards his sailors), but the young man loved the sea and to discover new towns. So far, he had been to Philadelphia, New York and even Boston. In his last letter, he had been very excited for their next trip to Charlestown, a new city in the south of the colonies. Vivien, who had never been further than Georgetown and its surrounding area, spent hours imagining what Michael was seeing. He made her dream of travelling, maybe by boat, and going to wonderful new places.

After Michael had left and Vivien cried herself to sleep every night, she confided in Judith about the marriage proposal. Her sister was happy for her (and not very surprised) but advised her to win over the Tanners whilst Michael was away, so they would not face the obstruction of his parents. Going against her best judgement, Vivien agreed to stay at home with her sisters and become a homemaker. She knew already how to take care

32

of the animals and sew, but Judith spent hours teaching her how to cook and clean properly. This training was made even more intensive as Judith got married on November 1686 and left the house, leaving Vivien in charge. It did not go down well with her twin sisters, who, though younger, spent their lives preparing to become the mistresses of the household. They had to strike a deal: the twins would take care of the cooking and the house, Vivien the animals and some sewing when necessary.

The fragile balance was disturbed again when Garrett got married in April 1687. His new wife, Joan, insisted on taking care of everything by herself until they had their own house. Fuming, the twins grudgingly agreed but retrieved the care of the animals and the orchard. Left with almost nothing to do, Vivien asked if she could go help her parents and brothers in the fields. The work was hard, but it kept her busy and safe from JJ's reprisals – even though she must admit that after so many years, it would have been odd for him to still be mad at her. On Sunday the family went to church and Vivien truly made an effort to look like a potential daughter-in-law: she asked Joan to help her tidy up and groom her hair, and her sisters helped her sew a nice and unpretentious dress. The wild girl had turned into a pretty and modest adolescent, polite and hard at work. She started to stir boys' and men's attention, and she did not like it. Vivien never did anything to encourage them and always managed to go to town with one of her brothers to avoid unwanted attention. She ended up telling her parents about Michael's proposal; they were not thrilled but they agreed that he was from a good family and would make a good husband, so her father refused all other proposals for her hand.

During that busy time, Vivien did not forget the Tanners. Once or twice a week, she would wear her old attire, take her bow and go hunting. As if Michael was still there, she would send one of her brothers to the Tanners' farm with half the meat she had killed. Every Sunday after church, the Tanners came to her to thank her for the meat and talk a bit. They were kind people and always had a nice word for her. By then, JJ was married and his wife was with child; the second son, Paul, was engaged and would be married in the spring; and Charles was desperately in love with Vivien. It was always strange for her to see him as he looked so much like Michael: the same nose, jawline, smile and freckles. A couple of time he had caught her staring at him, and she was afraid it had reinforced the idea that she also had feelings for him…

The last Sunday of January, the Tanners came to church wearing black stripes on their arms. The mother's eyes were red and puffy, and the rest of the family was barely better. The father went to talk to the pastor and before the beginning of the mass, he announced that Michael was dead. What happened after, Vivien could not say. She did not faint – at least not immediately; her body did everything that was expected of it as if it had a life of its own. When she came back to her senses, she was lying on the bed she shared with her sisters, the twins watching her. Ann went up and ran to fetch their parents, whilst Beth gave her some water.

"What happened?" asked Vivien with a hoarse voice, so far from her own.

Beth did not answer. Soon they heard heavy footsteps and their parents came in the room. Each sat on one side of the bed, looking uneasy. Beth went out of the room.

"What happened?" repeated Vivien.

Her parents exchanged a look, before her mother answered, "We were at church and we heard the news. You were fine until we arrived home and then you fainted. You scared us."

"I don't remember anything… What news did the pastor announce?"

Her parents tensed and this time, it was her father who spoke. "Michael's death."

Vivien closed her eyes, tears rolling down her cheeks. She could feel her parents squeezing her hands in an attempt to comfort her, but it was not working. It never worked; what was a small, comforting squeeze compared to the loss of a loved one?

She took a breath. "How?"

Puzzled, her father asked, "How what?"

"How did he die?"

"I don't know; they did not say…"

Vivien opened her eyes. "I must know. I am going to talk to them."

Her mother opened her mouth to object, but her father silenced her by putting his hand on hers. "I'm coming with you, Vivien."

The girl nodded and they left the house, followed by the disapproving glance of Mary Kane. The day was cold and it was snowing; soon both father and daughter were drenched, but Vivien did not feel it. Her father tried to make conversation on the way to the Tanners' farm, but she did not answer; she could not answer, as the three words *Michael is dead* were running in her mind. The thought was hardly bearable and she did not know if she could – if she wanted – live in a world where Michael was not.

They finally arrived and Steve Harlock knocked at the door. After a minute or so, JJ's wife opened the door – Mary, Martha, Moira? Vivien could not remember. It did not matter anyway.

"Good evening, we would like to talk to Mr and Mrs Tanner."

Without even answering, the girl nodded and closed the door. After another wait, the Tanners came out – both their faces had traces of tears.

"Mr Harlock, this isn't a good time, as you already know, we would appreciate not to be disturbed—"

"I understand, Mr and Mrs Tanner, and I give you my deepest condolences for your loss, but—"

Vivien cut in, her head low, "What happened to Michael?"

Mr Tanner faced her, a furious look on his face. "I know you were his friend, but it does not give you the right to come in my house and make demands!"

Vivien looked up and said in a dull voice, "I was his fiancée."

Her answer was welcomed by silence, broken by Mrs Tanner's hysterical laugh. Her husband tried to calm her, without success.

"Do you think because you wear a dress and send us meat we will believe you? Michael would have never married you. He had a bright future in front of him and he was going to marry a girl from a good family. Not you!"

Mrs Tanner broke into manic sobs. Vivien was shocked and she could see her father clenching his fists at such derogatory remarks. The Tanners were wealthier than them but not much better. Vivien put her hand on her father's arm to calm him; he glanced at her and relaxed a bit.

"It doesn't matter what you think of me, but I beg, please tell me what happened to him," pleaded the girl.

Mr Tanner shook his head. "It won't change anything. Do not come back."

Without saying goodbye, Mr Tanner opened the door and dragged his sobbing wife inside. The Harlocks were left on the porch, trying to process the scene.

"I would have never pegged them as being so conceited," started Steve Harlock.

Vivien nodded, but before she could answer a silhouette came out of the shadows at the side of the house.

"Good evening," said Charles Tanner timidly.

The Harlocks nodded in response. As the silence grew and nobody moved, Charles cleared his throat and added, "Michael had told me about the two of you before he left. I'm sorry for your loss."

Reassured by the kindness of the young man, father and daughter relaxed.

"Thank you," answered Vivien. "I am sorry for your loss too."

Charles nodded, briefly too overwhelmed to reply. "Sorry, I just cannot believe that I will never see him again…" His voice broke and tears started to stream down his cheeks. Vivien came closer and put a hand on his arm. She asked in a soft voice, "Can you tell us what happened?"

37

Charles nodded, took a deep breath and explained, "They were coming back from Charlestown fully loaded when pirates attacked them."

Mr Harlock opened his eyes wide. "Pirates? Near our coasts?"

"Apparently it isn't very frequent… It was the Ghost…"

Mr Harlock whistled. "I've heard of him."

Surprised, Vivien shot a side glance at her father. She had never heard of that man before. "Where?" she asked.

Her father shrugged. "At the tavern. He is a bad pirate, maybe even the worst. He is also the best: he had been skimming the ocean for a few years or so, but no one knows who he is or where he is from…"

Vivien frowned. "How so?"

"He rarely leaves survivors. It is very difficult to know how many ships he has attacked over the years."

The girl had become whiter than before. She used the wall of the house to support herself. "How do we know it was him then?"

"One of the sailors survived – well, he jumped in the water as soon as they noticed the Ghost coming for them. They were close enough to the coast that he managed to swim to safety."

Vivien smiled bitterly. "A coward then."

Her father nodded. "Yes, a coward, but a coward alive."

She closed her eyes and blamed Michael for being so responsible and brave and not thinking to survive for her.

Charles carried on telling the story, his voice regularly breaking. "From afar, he saw the boarding and the battle. Before they left, the pirates took the shipment and shot with their cannons until the ship sank. He waited for a day on the shore but nothing else other than broken wood and dead bodies were brought by the waves…"

Silence followed this. Charles and Vivien were both crying, holding each other's hand.

After a few minutes, Mr Harlock cleared his throat. "Thank you, young man, for speaking to us. We are grateful for your frankness. Vi, let's go home, your mother must be worried. Good night, Charles."

Vivien nodded and waved goodbye as she was still unable to speak. Charles stayed outside long after the silhouettes of the Harlocks had vanished in the darkness.

THREE

August 1690

The days went by smoothly. Alix had never been so happy as she was in her new family: she had a sister who loved her, a fiancé who was handsome and kind, and a mother-in-law who welcomed her with open arms. With Marguerite, every day was an adventure; they would sit with the rest of the family for meals and then had the rest of the day for themselves. In the morning, they would explore the castle – or rather Marguerite would test Alix's sense of direction: could she find the way to her room from the East Tower? Or the North? These exercises were taxing for the girl but really helped her to understand how to move in the castle and where to go. The afternoons were spent exploring the surroundings of the compound: going to the beach, walking in the fields, having a long walk in the small forest… They brought a blanket, food and drinks to sit in the shade and chatter for hours on end.

One day they went to explore a cove; a rumour said that there were pirates hiding in the caves. The girls were both very excited. Each holding a basket, they set their course and walked over the beach. Soon they removed their shoes and pulled up their skirts to walk in the cold water of the Atlantic Ocean. Compared to Paris, this was a dream for Alix. She looked at the endless water, melting with the sky, the seagulls flying around, the tall and majestic dark cliffs and the golden sand in between. She thought of her sisters staying indoors sweating as she was here, smelling the ocean and letting the sun kiss her skin – not too much, however, so as to avoid a tan – and she laughed. She did not realise how unhappy she had been in her previous life, but now she felt so elated, so joyful at how her life had turned around.

Marguerite looked at her, "What's happening?"

Alix shook her head, smiling. "Nothing – everything is just perfect."

Marguerite rolled her eyes. "You are such a city-dweller!" She made a grand gesture. "This is just normal. It has been here my whole life, and it will still be here long after I pass away."

Alix smiled, amused. "Or maybe you just stopped looking…" Without giving to her friend an opportunity to answer, she started to run. "Race you to the cove!"

Startled, Marguerite stayed in the same place for a few seconds before shouting, "You don't even know where it is!" She then started to run.

"Somewhere in front of us!" shouted back Alix, laughing.

The girls arrived at the cove taking shallow breaths, from both running and laughing. They were so tired that they fell flat on the sand without even putting a blanket down first.

"I won!" commented Marguerite.

"Only because you pushed me," lamented Alix.

Her friend shrugged. "No, it was because I knew where I was going. Also I barely touched you – you tripped on something."

Alix turned towards her, falsely outraged. "Oohh, liar! You pushed me! I will wash your mouth out with soap."

Marguerite burst into laughter. "Please try – you will see what growing up in the countryside can teach you!"

Alix looked at her, intrigued and a bit scared. She knew by now that her friend could be wicked. She had never been one of her targets, and she was not ready to change that. She decided to change the subject. "Let's move and put the blankets down, it will be more comfortable."

"Yes, Your Ladyship," answered Marguerite mockingly, before adding, "Actually, I have a better idea: it is warm and we just ran – let's go for a swim."

Alix stared at her blankly. "I don't know how to swim."

Marguerite shook her head. "You Parisians really never learn anything useful. You will stay where you can walk."

On that point Alix could not really disagree, so she stayed quiet until she saw Marguerite undressing. Horrified, she asked, "What are you doing?"

Her friend stopped unfastening her dress and looked at her as if she was an idiot. "What do you think I'm doing? I am removing my dress to go in the water."

Her eyes widening, Alix whispered, "You want us to go *naked* in the water?"

Marguerite laughed. "You are so puritan sometimes! If I were alone, yes, I would go *naked*," she mimicked Alix's tone, "but we will go in our undergarments; they will dry quickly."

Alix hesitated a bit more, but she trusted her friend and since she had arrived at Beg Hastel, she felt more confident in trying new things. A bit nervous, she started to unfasten her dress. As soon as both girls were only wearing their long shirts, Marguerite started to run towards the water, slowly followed by Alix. The former carried on running until the water was up to her neck; the latter wet just her feet.

"It is very cold!" she exclaimed.

Floating, Marguerite looked towards her friend. "Stop whining! The ocean is always cold, but it's also invigorating. Come in, don't stop. Once you're in, it won't be that bad."

Not wanting to appear as a coward – even though she felt deeply tense – Alix took a deep breath, squared her shoulders, locked her jaw and started to quickly walk into the cold water whilst Marguerite chuckled. She only stopped when she arrived near her friend and smiled. "I did it, I am—"

Alix happy declaration was interrupted by Marguerite splashing her. Shocked, she stayed motionless. "Why did you—"

Once more, her sentence was cut off by another splattering, followed by Marguerite infectious laughter. This time, Alix decided not to let her friend win the round and splashed back. Immediately, the calm of the cove was replaced by shouts, splattering and laughter. Suddenly Alix stopped; she saw on top of the cliff a dark silhouette that sent a cold chill down her back. She opened her mouth to attract Marguerite's attention, but her friend, taking advantage of her distraction, tripped her and made her fall in the ocean. When Alix managed to stand again, coughing and her heart beating fast, the silhouette had vanished and she was more interested in getting revenge from Marguerite.

Sometime after, lying on their front, the two girls were drying out on the warm sand. There was a fresh wind and the sound of the ocean was like a lullaby to Alix's ears.

"Tell me about your family," asked Marguerite abruptly.

Alix turned on her side to face her friend and answered prudently, "What would you like to know?"

Marguerite shrugged. "Anything. Start with your parents. Are they kind?"

"No, I wouldn't say that..." She turned to her back, her face facing the sky. "They were very strict... they are very strict. I was never allowed to do anything. Father would have an apoplexy if he ever knew I was going outside unsupervised, let alone swimming almost naked..."

"That sound absolutely dreadful," said Marguerite in a bored tone. "What about your sisters?"

"They were the same. So quiet, so obedient, so cold. I can't even remember an act of pure kindness from them." She turned to Marguerite, who was looking at her nails, took her hand and smiled. "You are much more of a sister to me than they ever were... and the Countess is also a much more compassionate parent than mine. I am very lucky to be with you."

Marguerite had a strange look on her face for a few seconds and then closed her hand around Alix's. "Oh, trust me, we are the lucky ones to have you. I've never had a sister and I would not wish for anyone else other than you to marry my brother."

Alix shot her a fond glance and Marguerite's smile turned wicked. "What about your brothers? You are very pretty; they must be good-looking too."

Alix blushed, partly due to the compliment and partly to see her brothers through the prism of handsomeness. Flashes of them came to her mind, how stuck-up and business-focused they were. She frowned. "I have never really thought of my brothers like that… Jean and François are very much like Father: tall, with dark hair and fair skin. They are both attending university. Maybe it is because they are my brothers, but I cannot see them as handsome."

"Isn't my brother very handsome? He also looks like Father with his blond hair and handsome figure."

Uneasy, Alix avoided answering the question. By now, she knew how to manage Marguerite, so she redirected the conversation. "What about your other brother?"

"Henri? He is tall and has blue eyes but has dark hair. Apparently he looks like his grandfather, but he could also be the son of the groom!"

Alix snorted in shock, increasing Marguerite's amusement.

"You cannot say that about your mother," cried a horrified Alix.

Marguerite shrugged and rolled her eyes. "I am joking. I am saying that because I know I can trust you not to repeat it to anyone; I had just hoped that you would appreciate my humour."

Calmed, Alix decided to play Marguerite's game. "I probably would have if I had ever seen that mysterious brother, but as that is not the case, I cannot comment or joke about him."

Her friend stayed silent, assessing the argument. "That is fair enough. I will make it again after you meet him." She smiled and winked at her friend, who could not help herself and laughed. After a short silence, Marguerite added, almost in a whisper, "I wish I had a fiancé who would take me far away from here and this life."

"What's wrong? You know you can tell me anything you want," asked Alix, concerned by her friend's unexpected seriousness and lingering sadness. As Marguerite stayed silent, she took her hand and squeezed it. "You can tell me everything – I am your friend and I will do everything I can to help you."

Marguerite turned towards her with eyes filled with hope. "Really, you would?"

Happy to have an answer, Alix smiled and squeezed her hand. "Of course! We are friends – no, sisters."

Marguerite sighed, stopping tears falling on her cheeks. "As you have probably noticed, Mother is particularly hard on me."

Alix nodded, though she had not seen anything specific. If she compared the Countess to her own mother, the former would always appear kind and caring. Yet she promised herself to be more careful with the way she interacted with others. "And I am not sure what the future holds for me. Louis will have a happy life with you, Henri will have a good career and I will stay home with Mother until I am old. No one asked for my hand, and I am almost seventeen! Do you think one of your brothers would be interested in taking a wife?"

Alix was not expecting that, and the image of the bubbly Marguerite with one of her stuck-up brothers made her laugh. This was not the reaction expected by her friend; furious, she got up quickly, took her clothes and started to walk back home. Realising her lack of tact, Alix rushed after her, taking her arm.

"Marguerite, stay, please—"

The girl turned violently and asked aggressively, "So you can laugh at me again? No, thank you."

Surprised at such a visceral reaction, Alix released her arm. She shouted in response, "I was not laughing at you! I was laughing because it is preposterous to imagine someone as kind and funny as you with one of my boring brothers. They follow the rules and they obey our father in every way. If that is the life you want – locked in the house, forbidden to do almost everything, subjected to a family who will destroy who you are – then I will write to Father tonight."

Both girls were surprised by the outburst, Alix more than Marguerite. Never in her life had she behaved like that or said those things about her family. She felt ashamed and intoxicated at the same time. She was brought back to reality by Marguerite talking.

"That's true? Your family is that bad?"

Alix nodded, unable to talk – saying out loud what she felt about her family made her tearful and strangely liberated. Marguerite hooked her arm around Alix's and went back to their things.

"I will have to find another husband then, ideally one without an overbearing family."

"But wealthy."

Marguerite rolled her eyes. "Of course wealthy, silly, that's a given!"

They both giggled and Alix added, "Then I will use all my might to find you a suitable husband!"

September 1690

Days later, Marguerite had decided that Alix would learn how to ride a horse. Her father had always refused that her and her sisters learned as it was, in his opinion, 'unbecoming of a lady'. As no one had ever challenged her father's decision – and she was not even sure that he could distinguish her from her sisters – Alix decided it was better to obey until… until what, she could not know at the time, but she was happy to never have angered her father or he would not have send her here. Every morning and night, she thanked God in her prayers to have brought her to this kind and welcoming house.

That morning, the two girls were standing outside the stables, Alix nervous and Marguerite more excited than usual.

"Noël, are you here?" shouted Marguerite as they entered the building.

A few seconds later, a man came out of one of the boxes; his size was average with large shoulders and impressive muscles. His skin was tanned, his hair black and his eyes brown. His face was neither young nor old.

"Lady Marguerite, what can I do for you?" he asked, looking at her with an intense gaze that made Alix slightly uncomfortable.

"Lady Alix would like to learn to ride."

The man nodded and turned his gaze towards Alix, slowly looking her up and down as if trying to memorise her figure – an attitude that made her feel even more uncomfortable. She frowned and he stopped his inspection. She looked at Marguerite but she did not seem to notice anything strange; she was innocently smiling. *It is in your head, Alix – you always*

48

expect the worst from people, just as your parents taught you, and they were wrong! She scolded herself.

Noël went to a box and, a few minutes later, brought a cream-coloured mare already saddled. "This is Nettle – she is kind and patient, so you have nothing to worry about with her, Lady Alix!"

Until then she had not been anxious, mostly excited to finally ride a horse, but his words made her wonder, what could happen? She could fall and look like an idiot, or get injured or even die. Prospects, each more awful than the other, came into her head. Before she could voice her brand-new nervousness, Noël had taken her waist and propelled her onto the back of Nettle. Alix was shocked by such forwardness and how he did not even ask if she was ready to do it. Once more she glanced at Marguerite, who did not seem to find it abnormal. Whilst waiting for Noël to saddle Marguerite's horse – Goldie – Alix got a feel of what it was like being on a horse. She put her feet in the stirrups and stood up slowly to check their resistance; she sat more comfortably and held the reins tighter; she looked around, seeing the world from a different point of view, and smiled. She felt like she was growing up, like life had so much to offer; she pondered how funny it was that a few minutes before she had been scared of mounting the horse and that now she deeply enjoyed being on it and the perspective it gave her. Marguerite's voice woke her up from her daydream.

"Let's go!" She gave Goldie a little kick with her heels and the horse started to walk.

Alix decided to do the same and Nettle followed. She held the reins firmer, her heart beating fast, but her apprehension did not last and she started to smile with all her might. She kicked again to go a bit faster and arrived at Marguerite's left side.

"Enjoying the ride?" asked the girl, her hatless hair shining like gold in the sun. Alix thought that the vision was actually striking: white skin with blonde hair, wearing white on a cream horse. She looked like an angel. She shook her head.

"Yes, I do, it is truly marvellous! I wish I would have been allowed to try earlier; this is so freeing."

Marguerite had a crooked smile. "We are just walking... What if we tried something a bit more dynamic?"

Alix frowned. "Such as?"

"Such as a slow trot." Feeling confident, Alix nodded vehemently. Marguerite smiled in approval. "So, sit tall and straight, always keep your eyes in the direction you want to move and flex your ankles so that your heels are lower than the balls of your feet." She looked at Alix's pose. "That's good. We will start the trot with a light kick and then you will have to rise and descend, all as lightly as possible. Is that alright?"

Alix nodded and both girls kicked their horses and they increased their pace. The speed surprised the inexperienced girl and she had to catch her saddle in fear of losing her balance. After a few minutes, her thighs were burning but she felt confident enough to release the saddle. Focusing on Marguerite leading the way, she still took some time to admire the scenery of slightly sun-burned green meadows, green leaves of various forms and the blue sky sprinkled with light-grey clouds... They rode for some time, entering an undergrowth and stopping at a clearing. Even though she was enjoying the stroll, Alix was grateful to stop and rest as she had never so much exercised in her whole life. Looking at how Marguerite dismounted, she imitated her with a groan. Being back on her feet felt weird, but she was happy to be able to properly stretch her legs. They laid out the blanket in the shade, sat and started to enjoy the collection of food prepared by the kitchens whilst the horses ate some fresh herbs.

After an hour or so, it was time to go back home. They tidied everything and it took several tries for Alix to mount the horse – to the great pleasure of Marguerite, who was making fun of her. By the time they were out of the undergrowth, the sky was a menacing grey. Looking at it, Marguerite said, "We will trot straight away – rain is coming and maybe a storm, and they can be quite impressive here."

Alix nodded and, gritting her teeth, started to trot. Her legs were burning but the cold wind felt good on her skin, at least until the wind was so strong that she fell her hat flying from her head. Lightning adorned the sky.

Marguerite came to her side, looking a bit scared. "We must get back home as soon as possible. A storm is definitely coming and we must be inside as soon as possible. So we will gallop – it will be quicker…"

Once more Alix nodded, this time not too sure what it meant for her. Marguerite did not need more and, giving a more vigorous kick to Goldie, the horse started to gallop at high speed. Alix did the same and immediately caught the saddle; it was fast and uncomfortable. The rain started pouring and she could not see where they were going – just the silhouette of her friend in the distance… a distance seemingly growing every time she looked. Alix was scared by the storm and the gallop, and even more by the prospect of losing Marguerite. She kicked Nettle to go a bit faster, but the opposite effect happened and the horse reared, throwing Alix on the hard floor. She rolled far away from the horse until trees and bushes stopped her. In the process, she hit her hip and her shoulder, and she fainted at the throbbing feeling of her injuries.

What awoke her was not the pain or the humidity of her clothing but the sensation of flying. She opened her eyes and saw that an unknown man had lifted her and carried her to God knew where. Her survival instinct kicking in, she struggled and started to shout. Though surprised, the man helped her to her feet and did not try to stop her when she backed away and picked a fallen branch from a tree as a weapon.

"What do you want?" she asked in a voice that was not too shaky.

The man looked at her without saying anything for some time, the silence only broken by the droplets of rain falling from leaves and the gusts of wind.

"A thank-you for finding you would have been enough," he finally answered with a tinge of amusement in his voice.

Alix looked at him, unamused. "Where I am from we don't thank kidnappers."

"You beat them?" he asked, pointing at the branch of a tree.

"Obviously," she answered with a smile that she hid immediately after. *A charming kidnapper, what a dangerous combination.* Especially for a handsome man. His hair was darkened by the damp, his soaked clothes had lost their colours, and yet Alix could see that his face had regular and handsome features, that he was tall and had broad shoulders. *He is strong too*, she thought. *He carried me without too much effort.*

"What's going on in your head?" he asked curiously.

"I am thinking you are a dangerous man."

He seemed surprised but did not deny it. "I am not dangerous to you."

Alix snorted – and immediately felt guilty, almost hearing her mother telling her that such behaviour is absolutely unladylike. "A sentence said by every dangerous man since the dawn of time!" She opened her eyes wide, bewildered. What had come into her? Since when did she have such wit and boldness?

Even though he did not laugh, the kidnapper could not repress an amused smile. "I meant you have nothing to worry about and, before you remind me of the poorness of my argument, I must add that I am Henri de Kerhoët."

"Oh."

"Oh indeed. Maybe you could drop your weapon and we could go back to Beg Hastel—"

"How do I know that you are who you say you are? Why did my fiancé not come look for me?"

Henri shrugged. "I was already soaked and he does not like dirty clothes."

Alix looked at her sundress, all muddied and covered with dead leaves and pine needles. "He couldn't know I would be that... unladylike."

Henri did his best not to laugh at her understatement. "He is not the most courageous man."

"But you are?" she answered sarcastically.

"No, but I did not think a muddied little girl would be a threat."

Alix felt both humiliated and furious; tears came in her eyes, but she refused to let them spill over. "Fine, let's walk back to the castle."

"I have a horse."

"I prefer to walk, but please, go back on your horse."

Henri sighed heavily, grabbed his horse bridle and started to walk, followed by Alix still holding her branch.

They arrived at Beg Hastel in the early evening – as soon as she saw the castle, Alix threw away her weapon, which made her future brother-in-law laugh. She was about to tell him off when she saw something unusual in the night. She kept on walking, trying to pinpoint what had attracted her attention. There was the castle, its towers and some light at the windows. Then her heart missed a beat: one of the lights was at the top of the North Tower, the forbidden tower. She grasped Henri's arm, making the young man shoot her a curious look.

"Why did—"

Alix did not let him finish his sentence. Her gaze was still locked on the light, and she pointed her finger. "Look, there is light at the top of the North Tower." She tore her gaze from the castle to Henri, just in time to see his facial expression change. She could not say what it was – sadness, fear, anger? Maybe all of these, but it was gone in mere seconds.

He shrugged. "I don't see anything. Perhaps the knock on the head you received earlier has made you see bright colours. We will send for the doctor to examine you."

"I am fine," said Alix through gritted teeth, "and there is a light at the top of the North Tower."

Henri looked at her with pity. "Mother must have told you that the North Tower is in disarray. There cannot be a light there, as no one can go that high without fearing for their lives."

His logical reasoning and assured tone made Alix doubt. She glanced again at the tower, but the light was gone. Could she have imagined it? Her hand instinctively reached out the back of her head to check if she had any injuries. Through the wet mane of her hair she could not feel anything. No warm blood, no pain. Yet, there was no light and she was confused…

They finally entered the castle, where the Countess, Louis and Marguerite were waiting for them.

"Dear Alix, I am so relieved that you are safe and sound. We were all so scared when Marguerite came back alone!"

Whilst a crying Marguerite rushed into Alix's arms, the Countess elbowed Louis to do the same. Alix could not discern the expression of her fiancé, but she knew he was not keen on coming to check on her.

"I am so, so, so sorry, I did not realise that you were not following!" Marguerite managed to say through her tears.

The Countess rolled her eyes and said with a snappy voice, "Marguerite, stop smothering the poor girl. She almost died today – do not make her day worse with your whining!" The two girls exchanged a look, Alix squeezing Marguerite's hand whilst her friend calmed her tears. "I sent someone to fetch the doctor and Thérèse has a bath ready for you." Louise did not let Alix answer before making her leave the room.

The bath was warm and did make her feel better. The doctor did not seem to find anything wrong – except a few scratches and some building bruises on her hip and shoulder; she knew she was fine. Without eating anything, she went to bed early and fell asleep immediately.

The events of the day had taken a toll on her and Alix slept through the night until Thérèse woke her up for breakfast. She was well rested and ready to welcome whatever the day had in store for her. The storm was nothing more than a bad memory, the sun was high and bright, and the sky blue and cloudless. When Thérèse was brushing her hair, she noticed dark circles under her eyes and her face looked sad.

"Thérèse, are you alright?"

Without even glancing at her, the maid answered mechanically, "Yes, My Lady, I am fine. Thank you for asking."

Unconvinced, Alix tried again. "Thérèse, look at me." The maid looked at her. "Are you alright? You are not your usual cheery self."

Something briefly came through Thérèse's face, dispelled by a forced smile. "I am fine, I assure you. I… did not sleep very well. It won't happen again, My Lady."

She resumed her brushing. Alix stopped the motion by putting her hand on top of Thérèse's and waited for the girl to look at her. "We haven't known each other for very long, but I care about you, so if there is anything I can do to help you, to release your burden, let me know."

Thérèse had a sad smile. "This is very kind of you, My Lady, but I am fine and there is nothing that can be done to help me. I beg you not to worry."

Feeling that the conversation was over, Alix nodded and removed her hand.

A bit later, when Alix entered the dining room, she was surprised to see the table full. She did not connect Henri's sudden arrival to the Count and was a bit taken aback to see the patriarch of the Kerhoët family presiding at the table.

"Father is back." Marguerite beamed, looking adoringly at the man.

He looked like an older version of Louis: same blond hair, same blue eyes, same facial features and frame. The resemblance was uncanny, yet where Louis was soft, he seemed hard; where Louis was indolent, he seemed sharp. For no reason, the first word that came to Alix's mind when she saw him was cruel. They had not spoken; she had just seen him for mere seconds, but she felt as if something was off with this man. He stood and he was tall, at least a head taller than her – like Henri.

"Lady Alix, what a pleasure to finally meet you. Please accept my apologies for not having been here on your arrival – some business took Henri and I out of Brittany." He bowed and kissed her hand. Marguerite's giggles and the Countess's sharp glance gave Alix the impression that it was a charming gesture, but she felt uneasy. She decided to smile and bow her head.

"The pleasure is mine," she forced herself to answer.

The Countess gestured for the girl to sit and smiled warmly, "You scared us very much yesterday; we are all so glad that you are well. Isn't it such a relief, Louis?"

"Yes, Mother," answered the young man. He stretched his arm to take Alix's hand in his. "I don't know what I would have done if something happened to you. You must be very careful in the future, my dear."

Alix was very surprised by this statement, as over the past two months she had barely seen him outside of mealtimes. Every time she suggested for him to join Marguerite and herself on an excursion, he had an excuse not to come – a meeting with a sharecropper, looking at the finance of the estate or going for a hunt. They did not talk much and certainly did not have the opportunity to develop feelings for each other. *If he died tomorrow, I would not grieve him much*, she thought uncharitably, before silently chastising her lack of sensitivity.

"My dear, isn't she the cutest fiancée with her blush and her timidity?" asked the Countess to her husband.

Looking at Alix intently, the Count nodded before turning his attention to his younger son. "Is there something funny, Henri?"

"Of course not, Father, I was just smiling fondly at the happy couple."

To Alix's disbelief, no one seemed to notice the obvious sarcasm. She shot a glance at the man who was looking innocently at her, but it was fake; she knew it. Her dislike of her future brother-in-law increased; she did not know why he was making fun of her but found it deeply insensitive and hurtful. Luckily, they resumed breakfast as usual: Marguerite chatting, Louis mostly ignoring his fiancée, the Countess now engaging with her husband and Alix staying quiet, not sure yet how to fit in this family.

FOUR

May 1688

Months had passed since Michael's death and Vivien was still numb. She talked and moved as usual, but her mind was with him, in the depths of the ocean or rotting on a forgotten shore. She did not know and it bothered her. Her family could see that she was having a hard time coping, but they did not know how – nor did they have the time – to help her. Life went on and other worries came to their minds: the winter had been colder than previous years, Garrett and Joan had had a baby girl (the delivery was difficult and they both almost died; Joan spent the weeks after that in bed, leaving the caring of little Catherine and the house to the twins) and Patrick had gotten engaged to Emma, a girl with German roots (which did not go down well with their mother). Vivien was a spectator to those events; she stayed afar from life and its events, not engaging. The only time during the week when she became alive was after the Sunday mass, when Charles Tanner came to her. They sat for hours on a bench, holding hands, sharing memories of Michael and crying together. They helped each other in a way no one seemed to understand. Particularly not the Tanners, looking down on Vivien and scared she would capture the heart of another one of their sons.

One evening when Vivien went back home, a smile on her lips after a heart-warming conversation, Joan asked her, "After Michael, you're going to marry his brother?"

A deafening silence fell on the house, only broken by the wailing of Cathy. The members of the household expectantly looked at the two girls. No one could say if it was a genuine or malicious question. Vivien's face was white when she answered through gritted teeth, "Of course not, don't be ridiculous."

Vivien turned to leave the room, but Joan insisted, "Then why do you spend so much time with him holding hands and talking?"

Vivien looked up and saw her father, his eyes pleading with her not to make a scene. She took a deep breath and answered, "And crying, don't forget the crying part."

Oblivious to the atmosphere, Joan carried on. "They could be tears of joy after a proposal. He is of a good family and will assure you a good place in life."

After that, Vivien lost it. "I already knew you were selfish, but I never realised you were that stupid. My fiancé was killed a few months ago! What's wrong with you to even think that I want to marry his brother?"

Furious, Garrett intervened. "Vi, I do not accept you talking to my wife like that – apologise now!"

"But you accept that she speaks to me that way? Implying those awful things?"

Garrett dismissed her argument with a flick of his hand. "Please don't be so childish; she just asked a simple question."

Vivien looked at him coldly. "A simple question? How would you feel if something happened to Joan and people started spreading rumours that you're going to marry her sister? What about you, Joan? If something happened to Garrett, would you marry Patrick?" They both looked at each other, out of arguments. "That's what I thought – not so fun when it's about you… Next time you want to ask a stupid question, think about it beforehand."

Vivien turned to leave the room and was face to face with her mother, who looked at her, her grey eyes darkened by rage. The girl just had the time to utter the word 'Mother' before Mary Kane slapped her hard. Vivien was sent backwards and she lost her balance, falling heavily, her head bouncing on the wall. The last thing she heard before passing out was her father calling her name with a panicked voice.

Vivien woke up a couple of days later. Her head was banging, her body was stiff and weak from the lack of food. For the first time in her life, she was the sole focus of her sisters, even Judith, who came back every day to help take care of her. They helped her eat, wash and walk. The first day, it was just going around in the house, Vivien always insisting on doing more. The second they went outside, still staying close to the house – Judith did not believe that she really felt better. The days after they went further, up until Vivien's sisters all agreed that she was back to her normal self. That week was also the first time that Vivien had rested and not done any manual work, which gave her time to think about her future, what she wanted to do and, of course, Michael. Neither her mother nor her brother came to apologise. Everyone in the house acted as if nothing happened.

The Sunday came and Vivien was more excited to talk with Charles that she had ever been before. She had reached a decision about her future and she had to tell him; she did not have the same feelings for him as she had for Michael, but he was her only friend and she had to talk to him. Never before had mass felt that long to the girl; she kept on wiggling on the bench, to her parents' dismay. Finally, it was over and she went to wait for Charles at their usual spot. As soon as she saw him, a wide smile lit up her face, the first since Michael's death, which surprised Charles.

"How are you?" asked the young man. "I heard you had an accident and that you were unwell this week."

Vivien shrugged, not wanting to give any details. "I am fine, but I had time to think and I came to a decision."

Charles eyed her: she was eager; he knew something was up and his hopes were raised. Maybe she finally shared his feelings and was ready to tell him? Maybe Joan put a kind word in for him?

"What decision?" he asked.

"I am going to avenge Michael," she answered proudly.

The young man stayed silent for a few minutes, his hopes destroyed, unsure how to answer that. "How so?"

Vivien sat on the bench and gestured for him to join her. "I will go to Georgetown and get employed on a marine ship. I will learn how to sail, then hunt down the Ghost, kill him and sink his nefarious ship." She stopped talking, proud of her plan and herself.

Charles looked at her as if she was mad. "But you are a girl! You are supposed to get married and have children, not plan to murder someone."

Vivien stiffened, her smile leaving her lips. "It isn't murder; it's vengeance."

"Potato, potahto. Don't ruin your life trying to get some revenge." He took her hand. "If you get married and have kids, they won't have won. Michael would have wanted you to be happy."

Vivien took her hand back, happy to not have told him the full extent of her plan. She also realised that maybe Joan was not far from the truth – at least from Charles's point of view. It made her sad, as she thought she'd had a friend but had ended up with an unwanted lover.

She answered in a dull voice, her eyes fixated in front of her, "It does not matter what Michael would have wanted; I cannot be happy knowing his murderer is free, looting and killing innocent people. I must do something," she glanced at his sad face and felt obligated to add, "and then, maybe, I could be happy."

"Here?"

Vivien did not want to give him hope. Until now, she had felt that her home was here, but the incident the previous week told her that it was not true anymore. Her family was not an ally and they would not support her decision.

"If I leave, I don't think I will be able to come back, or rather, I don't think my family will forgive me," she answered truthfully. She tilted her head back, looking at the sky. "If I leave, it is to never come back, but I will let you know if I succeed."

They stayed silent for a long time, Vivien looking at the sky and Charles at the ground.

He finally asked, with an edge in his voice, "When will you leave?"

There was something in his tone or the intonation he used that made Vivien uneasy. She could not say what it was, but she had learned to trust her instinct when she hunted, and now her guts told her to appease him, to lie.

She turned her head towards him and smiled with affection. "Not soon. I need to prepare some clothes, food and put some money aside. Also I think it would be better if I waited for the days to be longer in June."

Charles nodded, relieved to have more time to convince her. "That seems like a reasonable plan."

Her smile became larger and she hoped he would not see how fake it was. After one last squeeze of the hand, she got up and joined her family to go home.

That same night, Vivien put dried meat, cheese and bread in her hunting bag; she had a small nest egg of cash, so she hid this in various places of her clothing. In the morning, she banded her chest and wore her hunting gear with the bow, the arrows and the knives. Her heart beating fast, she announced as naturally as she could that she was going to hunt that day and her parents agreed to it. Not long after dawn, the girl was on the road to Georgetown. After a few miles, she undid her hair and without second thought trimmed her long dark mane for a manlier haircut.

The town was of decent size, but for Vivien, who had never been outside her farm and village, it was massive. Her eyes opened wide and she looked at everything: the people, more than she had ever seen in one place; the shops, so many more than back home and with so many products; the streets, with their passers-by, the horses and various carriages. She was even more amazed when she arrived at the port and saw for the first time the ships. The galleons were so much bigger than she expected, discharging their shipment or waiting for a new one. She stayed for a few minutes in awe of the beautiful constructions, before focusing on her task. She enquired where the ships were going and decided to try her luck with the *Princess Anne*, a four-mast galleon that was going to the Caribbean. From what she heard from her father, this was the place where pirates went. She was aware that she did not have a specific location, but once she was on one of the islands, she could carry on research. Whilst the sailors were charging the shipment, Vivien asked if they were in need of a cabin boy. The sailor looked at her with a grin and indicated a tall and large man, the second. She went to him and repeated her question. The second looked at her up and down.

"What's your name, boy?"

Vivien was so relieved that he thought she was a boy that she almost forgot to answer. "Victor, but everyone calls me Vi."

"How old are you?"

"Thirteen, sir."

He considered her as if he did not believe her. "You are small and frail; you will not be very helpful here. Go bother someone else."

Furious to see her plan collapse so quickly, Vivien followed him. "I might be small but I ain't frail. I am hard at work and I don't complain much. Give me a chance."

The second had an amused glimpse in his eyes. "We are going to the Caribbean if you don't fit what will we do with you?"

"You could leave me there."

The second laughed. "Fine, Vi, you are hired." He paused. "However, if your work isn't satisfactory, we won't wait until the Caribbean to disembark you…"

Vivien forced herself to show no emotion, earning a small nod of approval from the second.

"Monroe, show our new cabin boy his hammock on the below deck, then check if the captain needs anything before the departure; we have only a few hours before sunset to finish embarking the shipment."

The days on the *Princess Anne* were monotonous, long and tiring. As cabin boy, Vivien spent most of her days running errands for the captain, Robert Johnson. He was a kind man but always needing something or wishing to talk to someone, so Vivien was running around. Before the meals, the second always managed to grab her and send her to help the cook – this was probably her least favourite task. A few times a week – or when she did something to annoy the second – she would scramble up the rigging into the yards. Very occasionally, she was sent to stand watch or act as helmsman when the weather was good, holding the wheel to keep the ship steady on her course. Vivien enjoyed doing those things; she felt like she was living the words Michael wrote to her and that it was where she belonged. She could not say why, but she felt good on the ship, even when she was doing some chores. She enjoyed the way the ship was moving, the smells of the ocean (a bit less those of the sailors in the forecastle) and the sounds around – the sails, the birds, the creaking of the ship… all of it. Despite her loss, she felt good and happy for the first time in months. Several times, she dreamt that Michael was with her, smiling, blessing her decision.

As she was the newest crew member, the others were a bit wary of her. She did not understand why exactly, but often conversations would stop when she arrived. Vivien did not mind not being forced to talk and socialise, but she found that odd. One day, one of the youngest sailors sat with her for dinner; she pretended she did not see him.

"Hi, I'm Francis."

He was a tall boy, but, seen close, Vivien could see that he was young, maybe younger than her. His hair was brown, his skin tanned and his eyes light brown too. If she had seen him in the village, she would have thought he looked nice. Yet, she was on a ship where she did not know anyone. Vivien grunted, a bit annoyed to have to answer; she was afraid of some reprisals if she did not engage.

"Victor, but they call me Vi."

Francis laughed. "Sounds like a girl's name."

Vivien stared blankly at him until he started to wiggle. "Sorry. I kind of forgot how it was to talk with people."

A bit surprised, Vivien asked, "What do you mean? Aren't you a member of the crew? They talk together, don't they?"

The boy shrugged. "I don't think they trust me. I've been on board only for a few months; I was the cabin boy until you came. They don't really talk to me…"

"Why?" asked an intrigued Vivien.

Francis hesitated and came closer, whispering, "They are bit dodgy…"

Before he could finish his sentence, a shadow surrounded them and a voice boomed, "Boys, what are you talking about?"

Both Vivien and Francis jumped and distanced themselves from each other. The shadow was Richard 'Dick' Smith, a sailor in his late twenties, tall, with large shoulders and almost no neck. He smiled maliciously, which showed a few teeth missing.

"Hey, kiddos, what are you talking about?"

Vivien felt the threat in his words, tone and body. She also knew that the other sailors had stopped talking and were looking at the scene, eagerly waiting for some action. It sent a cold chill down her spine, yet she was not one to go down without a fight. She straightened her back, relaxed her shoulders and smiled innocently, forcing herself to talk excitedly like a child.

"I told Francis that when I was on the lookout the other day, I could see the coast of Europe!" She smiled more broadly. "You see, it's where my mama and papa are from. He is from a small town…"

Before she could finish her sentence, the sailor had turned and gone back to the others. They heard him say that she was an idiot, probably a simpleton, talking about her 'mummy' and 'daddy'. Vivien and Francis exchanged a worried look but did not say much after that. The situation, however, gave Vivien confidence in her original plan: find a way to go to the Caribbean and, from there, enrol on a pirate ship. In the meantime, she would keep her mouth closed, just saying the bare minimum.

June 1688

A few weeks afterwards, the *Princess Anne* entered the harbour of Port-de-Paix, the capital of the French colony of Saint-Domingue. The town was situated on the north-west coast, near the famous island of Tortuga, and Vivien could not stop herself from eying the former pirate lair. She had heard the sailors talk about it, how the French filibusters had been forced out of Tortuga by the British about twenty years prior. She knew they must be somewhere on the other islands, but she did not know where. As the ship came closer to the bay, she felt overwhelmed by the task at hand. So far her plan had worked well, but now she was going to be alone in an unfamiliar city without knowing what her next move would be. She became acutely aware that her planning skills had been quite poor and that she had no idea what the next step should be. Sudden shouts from the second brought Vivien back from her planning and kept the anxiety at bay, at least for the time being.

Using her for his errands had created a strange bond between Captain Johnson and her – or rather he got accustomed to having her around obeying his orders quickly. He relied on her and sent her in town to deliver some letters: one to his tailor, one to an inn and one to a merchant regarding his next shipment. When Vivien left, they had barely started to unload the ship and she did not understand how they could do it as she found the heat hardly bearable. When they were sailing, there was always some wind to freshen the atmosphere, but there, in Port-de-Paix, Vivien was sweating non-stop. She had never felt that uncomfortable. When he called for her, stopping her from helping to unload the shipment, Vivien was grateful. She followed him through the streets of Port-de-Paix; the city was in full expansion, wooden houses being built all over the place, people walking quickly in the streets and a foul smell of dejections and perspiration magnified by the soaring heat.

Finally, they arrived at a marketplace where a man on a platform was haranguing the public in French. Vivien did not understand at first what it was about until a first person joined him on the platform. It was an exhausted black man, barely clothed, with both his hands and feet shackled. The Frenchman talked again and some people in the crowd – including Captain Johnson – answered. That's when Vivien realised that she was at a slave auction and that the *Princess Anne* was bringing back slaves to Georgetown. She felt sick. More slaves were shown on the platform and sold, but she did not count how many were bought by the captain. One was already too many. What felt like hours later, the auction ended and they went back to the ship, followed by a long queue of slaves. In the streets, Vivien could feel people looking at them and she read accusation in their eyes. When they arrived at the *Princess Anne*, the second came to them.

"Was the auction good, Captain?"

Johnson nodded. "Aye, it wasn't too bad. I have three more tomorrow and the day after. It should be enough to fill the hold if the merchandise is of good quality."

The second turned to Vivien, wanting to assign her some work, but stopped when he saw the haggard look on her face, her white and moist skin and her shaking hands. He asked, "What happened to the lad, Captain?"

Johnson looked surprised and then glanced at Vivien. "Nothing, he's probably not fit for the weather here. Let him have some rest, he'll be better tomorrow."

"Aye, Captain."

Still not in her mind, Vivien went to the below deck and lay on her hammock.

She soon gave up on sleep and the chance to forget what happened. She could hear the slaves' chains on the wood, their cries and shouts. She wondered how the other sailors could act as if it was normal, as if there weren't human being enchained in the hold. The sickness came back, stronger than before. She quickly got out of the hammock and found a bucket to vomit in. This whole situation was worse than anything she had expected – actually, she never thought she would ever be on a slave ship. When Francis found her with some food, Vivien could not say how long she had been crying and holding on to the stinky bucket.

"Vi, what happened? Why are you crying?" asked Francis, sitting at her side.

She dropped the bucket and took his hand. "This is a slave ship." As Francis did not answer, staring at her with a blank face, she said again, "This is a slave ship. Oh my God, this is awful!"

Francis lowered his head but still did not say anything, which angered Vivien. Still sitting, she started to punch him on the chest. As if he had awoken, Francis dodged, stood up and pushed her back with a kick. Vivien heavily fell on her side and winced.

"Don't be a baby, Vi! They are barely human, just

merchandise barely good enough for the work assigned to them! Slaves or sugar, it's the same."

Holding her side, Vivien just stared at him. He snickered and she realised that he had never been that shy and nice boy; he was just a hardened sailor on a slave ship, not caring for anyone or anything.

"I brought your food, I hope you will have grown up by tomorrow," he added before leaving the below deck.

Vivien needed nothing more to make her decision. Feeling better from her resolution, she gathered her meagre possessions and put them with the food (luckily some bread and dried meat) in her bag. She sneaked in the ship's kitchen to take a bit more bread and an empty flask that she filled with water, then waited in her hammock until night fell. She knew that most men would go out to drink in an inn, so she waited for the sailors on watch to be distracted before she went back on shore.

Until the departure of the *Princess Anne*, Vivien stayed hiding in the outskirts of the town; she found a small forest and, even though the vegetation and animals were different, her old instincts kicked in. She could have stayed in the city, but she was not sure if her old crew would be looking for her. Her plan was to go back to the harbour and do the rounds of the inns, looking for pirates. On the third night in the forest, she heard noises and saw some lights: she was not sure, as she could not understand the language, but it looked like some armed men were following other people. As soon as she heard noise, she climbed up a tree and stayed there, hidden by the luxurious leaves. After some time, there were some gunshots and more running around as if the armed men were looking for something, or maybe someone. It lasted for a long time, but they finally left – Vivien could not say if they were successful or not. After that, she tried to get a bit of rest, but her uncomfortable position and the fear of being eaten by a snake – she saw a few and they were much bigger than those back home – kept her awake. She decided to move when she saw the golden light of the sun rise. She went down the tree and stepped on something soft; soon after she heard a whimper of pain. Hidden by branches and leaves, there was a man. He was somewhere between twenty and forty, with a tanned skin, drawn features and a bullet wound on his right side. His shirt was soaked in blood and his hair – ginger, maybe – was dirty and darkened by perspiration.

He opened his electric-blue eyes and, with a pained smile, said, "I guess I deserve that."

His voice was hoarse and his declaration ended up in a cough. Vivien hesitated for a second and checked if he had weapons. She spotted a knife on his belt and took it.

The man looked at her, intrigued but not fearful. "Are you going to finish me off, boy?"

She shook her head as she sat near him, ruffling in her bag to find the flask. "Not yet."

He laughed but this too ended up in a burning cough. Vivien opened up the flask and, holding his head, made him drink.

"Thank you…" The man observed her and, after reaching an internal conclusion, added, "Do you want to earn money?" As she left without her wages, Vivien nodded. "Help me get back to my ship and there will be a reward for you."

"In the harbour?"

"No, somewhere else."

Vivien's heart missed a beat. All that mystery and the fact that he was injured meant only one thing: that man was a pirate and he would bring her to his ship. She would find a way to join the crew and find the Ghost and kill him… She stopped her thoughts, hoping that the man did not notice anything, but he seemed too focused on the pain he felt.

"Alright, let's go to your ship."

Vivien helped the man get up, held him on his good side and, using a compass to guide them, they started to walk towards the pirate ship.

The sun was already high when they arrived at a river. They had walked slowly but steadily for a few hours and they both were exhausted. Every time they heard a noise, they hid in the vegetation, and they were lucky that no one seemed to be looking for them. Vivien helped the man sit, gave him the flask and used the water of the river to clean his wound. It was not bleeding anymore but oozed and started to smell a bit.

The man saw Vivien's expression. "Don't worry, kid, I'm hard to kill!"

Vivien shook her head. "That's truly not a concern of mine."

The man laughed and took another sip of water. "Once we are on board, they'll remove the bullet and tomorrow I'll be as good as new."

Vivien shot him a doubtful glance but did not add anything. The man moved his good arm towards her,

74

indicating that it was time to move. Exhausted, Vivien started to believe that he was really hard to kill. For a few more hours, they followed the river to its mouth and there, majestic, was the pirate ship. A galleon without a flag, its sails slowly moving with the breeze.

"Here she is, isn't she beautiful?" asked the man.

Vivien did not answer but wholeheartedly agreed. The man on watch must have been waiting for them and soon after a rowboat manoeuvred by two sailors was coming to shore. Silently, they took the man on board and let Vivien follow them. She was a bit intimidated; finally, she had found some pirates and they were quite scary. One of them was missing an eye and the other had several red and puffy scars on his arms and even his neck. On the boat going to the galleon, Vivien wondered if this was a good idea after all…

Once they arrived on the ship, they were welcomed by the whole crew, silently looking at them. Rarely in her life had Vivien felt such a heavy atmosphere; even the smug pirate she rescued did not look cocky anymore. She did not look around too much, but she noticed that there were some women and that crew members were black and white. She was a bit surprised but remembered what her dad told her: that pirates made their own rules. A man came closer. He was older than the rest of the crew with grey hair and a beard. He was not very tall, but he was wide, with large arms and a powerful neck. He had fair eyes, a blue so light that it almost looked white, currently flaming with rage.

"Evan!" shouted the man. "What is wrong with you? What don't you understand about 'laying low'? You're bloody lucky that we chose to stay – you don't deserve it!"

The said Evan looked like a kid caught stealing some sweets. It took everything Vivien had in her not to laugh.

"I'm sorry, Captain, I saw an opportunity and took it."

The captain rolled his eyes. "Stealing purses isn't an opportunity, it's petty theft!"

"Thief once, thief always!" shouted a man from the crew.

Vivien could not identify him, but the captain did, and he answered back, "Shut up, Bill – next time you come back drunk and fall overboard, no one will come to your rescue."

Members of the crew sneered.

"Evan, go to Pierre, he will check on your wound. Also, your grind for the next month is to polish the deck."

A black man came to help Evan move. The pirate captain then turned his attention to Vivien; there was no more rage in his eyes, yet the girl was scared.

"As for you, boy, thank you for bringing him here. I assume he promised you some gold; we will give it to you and let you go at nightfall before we weigh anchor."

The pirate captain turned to leave her be, but Vivien interjected, "No, sir, I don't want money."

The man looked back at her, his eyes carefully examining her. His inspection was so thorough that Vivien started to feel uncomfortable.

"Then what do you want?"

Vivien squared her shoulders, attempting to look self-assured and more impressive than she was. "I want to join your crew."

The captain stayed silent and she heard some low chuckles. "Nay, we are too busy to look after children. Go back to your parents."

"Give me a chance! If you aren't satisfied with my work

you can leave me at the next pirate harbour."

The captain observed her, intrigued. "Why do you so badly want to become a pirate, kid?"

"None of your business," she snapped.

Vivien felt a heaviness settle in her stomach: had she gone too far? Would they kill her for disrespecting their captain? But the crew members started to laugh.

"Let him stay, Cap, the boy has some guts."

The captain looked around and replied, "Is it how you all feel?" The crew responded with shouts of 'aye'. The captain nodded and turned back to Vivien. "Welcome on board the *Mermaid.*"

FIVE

September 1690–March 1691

The months had passed since Alix's arrival and the family had fallen into a new routine. Later in life, she could not recall what happened exactly during that time; most days blurred together. She had learnt to ride a horse and enjoyed it – the fear of the first time was quickly replaced by exaltation every time she galloped away. She felt free, freer than she had ever been, even if it was just for a few minutes. As during the summer, Marguerite and Alix kept going out in the afternoon, riding or walking; their outing got shorter and shorter as the weather got colder. When they had to stay in the castle, they explored every bit and piece of it – with the exception of the North Tower, that seemed to terrify Marguerite.

She grew closer to Marguerite and the Countess; they were both always so nice and warm with her... Louis was charming and looked after her but only during the meals; his schedule the rest of the time remained a mystery. Never did he offer for Alix to ride with him, or for them to go on a walk, or just to spend some time together. Thérèse kept on looking sick and sad with her dark circles, and her thinner and thinner frame. Every time Alix asked her a question, the woman clammed up and started to cry, each occurrence ending with Alix hugging her and Thérèse asserting that she did not deserve her kindness.

The Count and Henri were away for their business trips most of the time, coming back to Beg Hastel every two months or so. Alix found that very convenient as the Count was scaring her and she had developed an unwanted and humiliating attraction to Henri. She kept thinking about him, much to her aggravation, for not only she was engaged to his brother but the young man, who was barely older than her, wickedly enjoyed reminding her that she was just an annoying and borderline idiotic child. The most humiliating thing was not even his attitude but her own attraction to him, despite his behaviour and comments. Every time they were at the castle, Alix made her best effort not to engage, not to react, hiding her anger and barely speaking. Yet, she could not stop looking at him, looking for him and collecting every glimpse of the young man. Christmas had been a particularly difficult time as the whole family stayed together and mostly indoors until the new year. Her strange attitude got her a few comments from Marguerite, but she soon forgot about the incident.

With hindsight, the event that signed her fate, that started a chain reaction, was not her engagement but something that happened on an April night.

April 1691

The meal had been heavy that evening and Alix could not sleep. She tossed and turned, particularly agitated that night. Marguerite would say that it was the full moon that made her restless. That thought made Alix smile, but not long enough. She needed to move. She grabbed a lit candle, put on a pair of slippers and a dressing gown, and went to have a walk in the castle. More than during the day exploring the castle at night scared her, so she went outside, hoping that the chilly air of the night would make a difference. She walked a bit and then noticed some light coming from the stables, which was odd at this time of the night. She approached the building and entered, hearing the voices of a man and a woman. She came closer and recognised Marguerite and Noël – they were talking, laughing and making some noises that Alix could not define. Dreading what she would find, the girl silently took a few steps forward and saw the two lying naked on straw. She did not understand what they were doing, but she felt her cheeks burning and, as noiselessly as she arrived, she went out of the stables and back to her room. On her way back, she noticed that there was another light on top of the North Tower, at the exact same spot as in September, but her mind was too busy with what she had seen to think about the North Tower. Needless to say, the pain in her stomach was forgotten, replaced with thoughts of Marguerite and Noël…

She must have fallen asleep at some point as Thérèse woke her up at her usual time. Alix was tired and preoccupied after that sleepless night. For once the roles were reversed and Thérèse asked, "Are you alright, My Lady?" As Alix did not answer, too lost in her thoughts, Thérèse put a hand on the shoulder of the girl and said with a smile, "You can confide in me if you need…"

As you confide in me? Alix wanted to answer, but she did not. Thérèse was her friend and if she was not ready to talk about what bothered her, she could not do anything about it. She sighed, "After yesterday's dinner, I couldn't sleep so I went for a walk, to the stables."

"Ah!" answered Thérèse with a blank face and a neutral voice.

Alix looked at her, squinting. "What do you mean?" She stayed silent for a few seconds, realisation washing over her. "You know what I saw, don't you?" Thérèse shrugged. "What did I see?"

Knowing that Alix would not stop asking questions this time, the maid caved. "You saw Lady Marguerite having sex with the groom."

Alix stayed silent. *They were having sex, naked. That's what those noises were… I don't want to do that with Louis.* She shrugged.

"Why?"

"Why what?" answered Thérèse, puzzled.

"Why did they do that?"

The maid stared at her, in disbelief at such innocence. "You mean have sex?" Alix nodded. "Because they wanted to."

"How long has it been going on?"

Thérèse shrugged. "I have known since… last summer, but it might have been longer."

Alix frowned and stayed silent. "This does not make sense – the church says sex can only happen between married people and only in order to procreate…"

Thérèse could have told her that the purpose of sex in this case was for everything but the prospect of reproduction, but she did not have the energy to explain this to Alix. The girl was too innocent for her own good, too innocent for this house.

"Do you think he is forcing her?" asked Alix.

Thérèse looked at her strangely and barked a joyless laugh. "No, I've seen them once and that's not what a forced relationship sounds like."

"How do you know?"

Thérèse shrugged. "If someone is taking advantage of another, it is Lady Marguerite. If the Countess heard about this affair Marguerite would be punished, but Noël would be fired and maybe even sent to prison."

Alix opened her eyes wide. "What do you mean? They cannot send him in prison for nothing."

Thérèse looked at her with a mix of annoyance and pity. "They are noble and wealthy – who do you think the judge will believe? The powerful Countess or a poor groom?"

Alix opened her mouth to answer but shut it immediately after. She closed her eyes and pressed her hand on her forehead, feeling a headache coming. *It's the shame of being so naïve, so stupid!* She breathed deeply and added, "Thank you for everything, Thérèse. Could you please let the Countess know that I won't be at breakfast? I am feeling a bit sick. No need to fetch the physician; it is just a headache, so I'll get some rest."

Thérèse curtseyed and left the room, feeling sad for shattering Alix's illusions. She thought of her own situation and decided that it was for the best – she was too naïve and needed to know the reality of life in order to be able to defend herself…

Alix lay in her bed, unable to find sleep despite her tiredness: too many thoughts were swinging in her head. *Why would Marguerite engage in an affair with a groom when her deepest desire was to have a good marriage? Was she lying about that? As she mentioned her wish to get married every day since I have met her, could she be lying about it? And why? It is true that she mentioned handsome men, but I did not pay much attention to that; I did not think it was serious… Also, if it is not for procreative purposes, why would she do that?* She remembered the sound Marguerite was making, as if she was enjoying herself. She blushed. *Pleasure, then… This is so immoral, and so is thinking about it!* Yet, Henri's face came to Alix's mind for a second and she blushed harder. Chastising herself for thinking of him, she went out of the bed to pray for God to save her soul and Marguerite's.

She was at dinner that evening, more silent than usual, observing the family members. They were all acting like usual, talking about uninteresting subjects. Her family had many defaults, but when they had nothing to say, they did not speak. She took a sip of her cider. Since she had arrived, she had been distracted by the constant chatter and the bubbly personalities of the Countess and Marguerite, but – and she realised it now – she did not know anything about them. They had managed to distract her enough to stop her from asking important or personal questions, and she did not understand why. In a year or so, she would marry Louis and become a member of the family. *Except if they have secrets to hide that might hinder, if not deter, me from marrying him.* She smiled in her glass at her own foolishness. *What could it be? Hidden bodies in the catacombs? Or worse, they are Protestants!* She smiled again, grateful that they all laughed at the same time at something Marguerite said.

"I am glad you are feeling better, my dear…" started the Countess. "You still look quite pale. Are you sure you don't need a physician?"

Alix examined Louise as she was speaking: her tone was kind and her facial expression appropriate, yet there was no warmth in her eyes. *How come I never noticed it before?* wondered Alix. She forced a smile. "Thank you for your kind concern – it is truly nothing. I've had it before; it is just a strong headache. I already feel better and will be back to normal tomorrow."

"I am so glad to hear that – we should have a ride then!" said Marguerite, and for the first time, Alix found her cheery tone unnatural; or maybe she was getting paranoid. She felt lost.

"Of course, I am sure I will be back to normal tomorrow and ready for an outing."

"This is a relief," added Louis with a bored tone before eating another piece of meat.

Was he always like that? Did I convince myself he was charming and courteous when he could not care less about my well-being?

They kept eating and, in spite of Marguerite's chatter, the dinner felt long and incredibly boring. The day after – and all the following – they were back to their old routine, but Alix could not shrug off the feeling that things were not normal and could not go back to normal anymore.

About a week later, after thinking it through, Alix was ready for a midnight trip to the North Tower. Since talking with Henri, she had not mentioned the light to anyone, yet it had been on her mind, and, since she had discovered that Marguerite was lying to her, she felt the need to know if that story was true or not. She had boots on her feet, her most comfortable dress, a cape, a knife and several candles. If there was something to find in this tower, she would. She went out of her room and through the corridors like a ghost – she knew the path; she had practised going there the quickest way possible. The door of the North Tower was off-limits – so Alix had looked around to find a side door and discovered that the basements were linked. Moving silently, she went to the lower ground floor of the North Tower. It was humid and colder than in the castle. She found some stairs and, prudently, started to climb them. On the ground floor, she looked around searching for any sign of disarray; there were none. As she expected, the small windows and the door were off-limits. The floor was large and empty. Examining it, Alix saw that there were footsteps, even a path, on the dusty floor. *People do come here. I hope it's not Marguerite and Noël – that would be a very embarrassing encounter!* she thought.

Taking a deep breath, she took the stairs to the second floor, where she went through every room. They were all empty and dusty, but there was nothing that led Alix to believe that it was on the brink of collapsing if she kept exploring. Confident in her intuition and even more motivated to discover the tower's secrets, she went to the third floor. Once more, there were no cracks or any other sign of disrepair. One more floor. Her heart was beating fast, her hands sweating.

She ran through the stairs, quickly looked into two open rooms and then stopped in front of a closed door. Through the cracks of the wood, she could see some light. Her mouth became dry and she knocked at the door – she could not say why she did it, but it felt right.

"Come in," said a female voice.

Alix swallowed and turned the doorknob. It was a bedroom, with a large bed, a sofa, a library and some odd furniture. Everything looked old. On a chair sat a young woman, who looked strikingly like the Countess. Her face was young, pale and beautiful; her long hair blonde; her eyes blue; she reminded Alix of the Madonna. She also noticed that she had an odd way to carry herself; it took a few minutes for her to realise that she had an uneven back.

"Who are you?"

The girl started to laugh. "Shouldn't I be the one asking you that? After all, you came uninvited into my room."

Alix opened her mouth to answer but nothing came out. This whole situation was unexpected; she did not understand what was happening and she was shocked.

Noticing her astonishment, the girl offered her a seat. "I am afraid I have nothing to offer you to eat or drink, except a drop of water. I am very glad to finally meet you, Alix Lecuyer, even though I believe it was not supposed to happen before the wedding, perhaps not at all."

"How do you know my name?"

The girl shrugged. "I live here – people talk to me. Also I saw you several times from the window; you have become quite a good rider. I wish I could join you, but I am not allowed to do so."

Alix shook her head and burst out, "Are you a prisoner here?"

The girl nodded sadly. "More or less, yes… My deformity would bring my family too much shame, so they decided to keep me away from their eyes and their thoughts."

"You are a member of the Kerhoët family?" asked Alix.

The girl nodded again. "I am Marguerite de Kerhoët."

Alix felt her heart miss a beat and became very white. *How can it be? It is impossible. They can't have…* Marguerite, seeing her angst, came to sit near her and awkwardly took her hand in hers.

Alix fought back tears and asked in a strangled voice, "How long have you been here?"

"As long as I can remember… Marie, my nurse, told me that they realised that I was different soon after my birth and put me here."

Alix felt ashamed for being so sentimental about being lied to, when the girl in front of her had been a prisoner for most of her life. She squeezed her hand back. "I am very sorry for what happened to you. Wait, who is the Marguerite I met? She looks so much like your father and brother…"

Marguerite had a sad smile. "Her name is Perrine. She is an illegitimate daughter that my father had with a maid. She was just about a year older than I and looked so much like the rest of the family that Mother had the idea of the exchange; I think it was also a way to take her revenge upon Madeleine – the maid – who was her personal maid before becoming my father's mistress…"

Alix was deeply shocked by what she had just heard. The lies, the immorality and the lack of charity of this family was making her sick. She stood brusquely and went to the window to get some air. This place, the family that a few months before felt so right for her had her now entrapped and bitter. She breathed deeply, fighting against the tears.

"I have also an older half-brother," carried on Marguerite, both because she needed to talk and because the silence was making her uncomfortable, "but Father sent him to the army when Louis got engaged with you. Baptiste was deeply unhappy to leave; if you ever meet him, I think he will be quite rude to you."

Hearing that, Alix could not stop herself from laughing. She turned and looked at a surprised Marguerite. "I have met one like that here – your other brother, Henri. I think I will deal with Baptiste the same way, by ignoring him!"

A strange look crossed Marguerite's eyes. "Don't be too hard on him – Henri is the only one caring for me in this family…"

Looking at the other girl, so sad and frail, Alix bit her tongue to stop a harsh answer; there was no need for them to argue. She smiled and came back to sit near her. "In that case, I promise that I will come to see you until I leave this forsaken place."

Marguerite, who started to smile at the declaration, fell serious again. "Leave? How do you intend to leave?"

"I was thinking to write to my father and tell him the truth."

Marguerite shrugged. "If he is any bit like my father, it won't make a difference."

"That's true, but my family is very religious, and what you just told me shows that your family is immoral and untrustworthy. Knowingly leaving me here would hinder his hope to go to Heaven… He will be annoyed at me and probably punish me in some way, but it will be better than being here."

"Is it that bad, downstairs?" asked Marguerite timidly.

Alix shook her head. "It is very pleasant, except when your father and brother are here, but I knew something was wrong and already discovered some disturbing truths. Knowing to what extent your whole family have lied to me these past few months turns fond memories into bitter deceits. Also I am quite relieved not to have to marry Louis."

"My brother is not to your liking?" teased Marguerite.

Alix looked at her out of the corner of her eyes, weighing up whether to tell her everything. *You've already said too much*, she scolded herself. She sighed. "Have you ever met someone who does nothing wrong, is polite and nice, but makes you uncomfortable?" Marguerite shook her head. "That's how I feel about him. Something bothers me, I cannot say what, but it is there. I tried to be kind, to engage with him, but he shows no interest in me, which just reinforces my negative feelings about him."

They stayed silent for some time.

"I should get back to my room now, but I will come back in a few days. Would you like anything?"

Marguerite's face lit up at the question. "Books, please! Anything that you can find. Henri brings me some every time he comes back home, but it is not enough to keep me company when I am alone."

Alix smiled and nodded. "I will bring you books then. Good night, Marguerite."

"Good night, Alix."

She closed the door, lighting a new candle to get back to her room, her head very confused by all that she had learned.

May 1691

The Count and Henri came back from another trip a couple of days after, so Alix could not go to see Marguerite. *The real Marguerite.* After almost three weeks, she still struggled to process all that had happened and all that she had learned; the more she thought about it, the more she felt – no, she knew – that there were more lies to uncover. She had written a letter to her father, sending it from a nearby village, as she feared it would be intercepted by the Countess if she sent it from Beg Hastel. What was more difficult was to pretend that nothing had changed, that she did not know. She had to laugh at fake Marguerite's jokes, be pleasant to her fiancé and the Countess. Some evenings, she felt tears at the corner of her eyes but forced herself to smile wider. Despite Marguerite, she had never been so alone in her entire life, and her mask was slowly cracking.

This whole situation also made her revise her view on God. She still believed in Him and realised that this whole situation was a trial of her faith and that if she went through it victoriously, she would earn her place in paradise. Yet she could not help but wonder: why her? Why could He not have let her lead a normal life, like the one she had had in Paris, atoning for incredibly minor sins? She wondered whether she would also have to atone for her new family's sins. She remembered her father mentioning that the sin of one family member became the sin of all of them. She was then doomed:

by all accounts, the Kerhoëts were sinners and, unless she went into a very strict convent, she would never be able to wash away their sins – especially as they probably would not stop being wicked, hiding their true nature. How could she atone for sins she was not aware of? The unfairness of the situation laid heavy on her, bringing more despair.

On the evening of the Count and Henri's return, they had a longer – and heavier than usual – dinner, to celebrate something Alix could not remember: a good business deal? Their return, perhaps? Or maybe they did not tell her. She was eating without engaging with the conversation, listening to their voices, trying to detect any form of deception. *Is this a real story? Are they faking their laughter? Did they even go on a business trip?* Even though Henri was here and she desperately wanted to look at him, knowing how deceiving the whole family was made Alix even more shameful of her attraction to the young man.

"Are you alright, dear? You are very quiet tonight," asked the Countess.

Alix was so lost in her thoughts that she did not immediately realise that this was addressed to her. She forced a smile to her lips. "I am well, thank you for asking."

All the family's attention was directed towards her; the Count in particular was looking at her intently, as if he knew that she had discovered their secret. She became anxious and her palms started to sweat.

"Good," answered the Countess, "yet you are still quieter than usual."

"She has been pretty distracted lately too," added fake Marguerite.

Alix kept her face as neutral as possible, but she knew her cheeks were becoming red. *Find something, any excuse to keep them unsuspicious.*

"I… I miss my family." She closed her eyes and did not have to put in much effort to shed a few tears. "I have not received a letter for a long time and I am worried about them…"

"Oh dear, I am sure they are well," answered the Countess with a compassionate mask on her face. Satisfied by the explanation, the rest of the family returned to their plates, indifferent to Alix's feelings. Only Henri kept looking at her; she ignored him and took another bite.

Alix had never felt more relieved at the end of a dinner. She used her family to excuse herself before the others. She was walking to her room when she heard footsteps behind her; she sighed and turned, ready to give more explanations to the Countess or fake Marguerite, but was startled to see Henri, a concerned look on his face.

Without preamble, he stated, "You know you can talk to me if you need to."

Surprised, Alix laughed, but she stopped quickly, seeing his serious face. "If I ever need to talk, you are certainly not the person I would go to," she snapped.

The fake concern and sympathy left Henri's face. "I was just trying to be kind, which I will certainly never do again."

Alix examined his face before shaking her head. "A few seconds of kindness does not make up for the rest…"

His face whitened but he quickly regained composure. Yet it was enough for her to be sure that he was as deceitful as the others and it hurt her.

"What do you mean?"

She could not say what she knew; even though Marguerite trusted him, she did not. Her heart beating fast, she shrugged and decided to be vague. "I think you know what I mean."

He stayed silent for some time until a smile appeared on his lips. She knew then that he thought she did not know anything; she felt relieved but did her best to hide it. He came closer and started to whisper in her ear, "You are a pretty idiot; you truly deserve my brother."

His words felt like a slap and Alix forced her face not to move, not while he was around. Looking straight into his eyes, she took a step back and turned, walking away at a normal pace. She wanted to run and cry, but she managed to control herself until she was in her room. Soon, however, the tears of humiliation turned into tears of rage. *How dare he treat me like that when his family is full of sinners? He is just as bad as them!* She took several deep breaths to control both her tears and her anger. Alix then had an idea: what if she went to spy on them? A rush of adrenaline came through her; she looked for her dark cape and went downstairs.

They were not in the dining room anymore. Trying to be as stealthy as possible, Alix went around and finally found them in the Count's office. The door was ajar, so she stayed on one of its sides and listen to the conversation. At first they did not talk about her and she did not really understand what it was about; they mentioned some trips, a booty and some gold. None of this made sense in what Alix knew about the family.

She was about to leave when she heard her last name: "We received a letter from Monsieur Lecuyer last week: he wants to break off the engagement," cautiously started the Countess.

There was a small silence and Louis answered eagerly, "I would be very happy about that, Father, I certainly do not want a wife and especially not one like her – she is—"

He was interrupted by the Count. "How dare that insignificant merchant request such a thing! We lowered ourselves in taking his daughter and making her a part of our family, not the other way around."

"Father, she is rather dull—" carried on Louis.

"It is true that she is quite a bore," agreed the Countess. "Our son deserves a less religious wife, someone with sparkling conversation and a good sense of fashion."

The Count cut off their rambling again, "Why does the merchant want to break off the engagement?"

Alix gritted her teeth, hearing her father's profession used in such a derogatory way. She remembered her fear of arriving in an elitist family; she smiled, realising that it happened without her knowledge.

"Well, he argues that we lied about our family, which annuls the contract."

The Count snorted. "How so?"

"It seems that he was made aware of your bastards," answered his wife with a honeyed voice.

"And? It is common amongst nobility."

"Not amongst merchants and especially not when they are Jansenists."

Alix heard the scraping of a chair. "Bloody Jansenists, there is a reason our King, and even the Pope, declared them heretics! These people truly are a pain in the ass."

Another silence followed the Count's outburst, broken by the Countess. "He also appears to know about Marguerite's... problem, and the small trick we are using."

"How could that have happened? Who could have talked?"

No one replied, but Henri spoke. "I don't see what the issue is: none of us like that girl, she is obviously below our standards and she does not fit within the family. What stops us?"

"The money, dear. Her birth might be low, but her pockets are full and we desperately need money."

"But all our trips are successful—"

The Count chimed in, "We need clean money – more specifically, her dowry. Of all those merchant families desperately wishing to rise in society, hers is the wealthiest. No, this marriage must happen... just earlier than expected."

"When?"

"Next weekend. None of her relatives would have the time to arrive. When they learn about it, it will be too late."

"And her dowry will be ours," rejoiced the Countess.

Hearing that, Alix realised that none of them could be saved. There was no point in praying for their souls; they were going to Hell. Despite the horror of what she heard, that insight made her feel better: she could not do anything for them. The only solution was for her to save herself and her soul by getting away at all costs.

"I really don't want to marry her," complained Louis.

"Sweetheart, don't worry, it won't have to be forever. Let her give you one or two heirs and then we will take care of the problem."

"Just one, Mother. I don't think I will have the patience to pretend to like her for longer—"

Before the Countess could say something, Henri interjected in an angry voice, "Are you seriously planning the murder of Alix? Are you that heartless?"

He did not let them answer; he opened the door and burst out. He immediately spotted Alix, frozen in place, grabbed her arm and dragged her with him. She had no choice than to follow, almost running to keep up with his quick and furious pace.

When they were almost at her room, he stopped in a corner, pushed her back towards the wall and whispered angrily, "What were you doing?"

At loss for words, Alix did not answer. *Isn't it obvious?* she wondered. Even more annoyed by her lack of response, he added, "Do you know what they could do to you? They could hurt you!"

This fake concern revived Alix's own anger. "I am aware of that; after all, weren't you planning to force me into marriage and then murder me?"

Henri clenched his teeth. "You are engaged to my brother; that part is going to happen anyway."

She shook her head. "I wrote to my father requesting to break off the engagement; I refuse to be a part of this family. One way or another, I will leave this place."

Henri looked surprised and relieved. Out of nowhere, he put his right hand on the side of her neck, inched his face closer to Alix's and kissed her hard. Her head bumped the wall, but she was too astonished to register the pain. After a minute or so, he stepped back with a strange look on his face. For Alix, it was the last straw and she slapped him hard.

"Never do that again!" she hissed.

Henri's face went from shock to delight, as he started to laugh. "I should have expected as much from a girl who threatened me with a tree branch!"

His thumb caressed her cheek and she shivered but refused to get side-tracked. "I am leaving tonight."

Immediately becoming serious, Henri nodded and added, "Good, but don't go back to Paris; they will look for you on the road."

She shook her head. "I don't have anywhere else to go."

"You could go to Lorient and embark on a ship for the Americas. I have some friends in New York; they would take care of you."

Alix looked at him, bewildered. "Why would I do that? I can find shelter somewhere in France and send a letter to my family."

Henri shook his head. "My father is a bad man and he is well connected. Your family will be monitored and their mail probably opened. You are not safe in this country."

"But I will be in another one, where I know no one?"

"My friends will take care of you…" He hesitated and timidly added, "And I will find you when you are safe."

Alix stayed silent, not sure what he meant. Too many thoughts ran through her head. *Is the Count that dangerous? Will he put my family in jeopardy? Despite everything, could I bear the idea of hurting my family?* She did not have much time and had to take a decision quickly, so she nodded.

Reassured, Henri kissed her forehead. "Go back to your room, change into your riding gear and take all the valuables you can find. Go out as discreetly as you can and meet me outside the compound in about half an hour."

Quickly, she went back to her room, a bit stunned by all the new information she had discovered that night. She did her best to focus on the task in hand and not the prospect that Henri might like her too – it was too distracting. Yet, despite the disturbing news she had heard tonight, she felt happy. She had changed and was packing her coins and jewels into pouches to hide in her clothes when she heard the door. She turned and saw Thérèse.

"My Lady, I just came to check if you needed anything before going to sleep." She looked at Alix's outfit and what she was trying to hide. "Are you leaving?"

"Please don't say anything," burst out Alix.

"What happened? Did Lord Louis do something wrong?"

Alix was about to answer when the oddly specific question struck her. She frowned and approached Thérèse. "Did Louis hurt you?"

The maid became red and nodded slowly, lowering her gaze. Alix hugged her, thinking that every time she thought this family could not be worse, she discovered a new horror.

"I am going to the Americas, where they will not find me. Would you like to join me?"

Thérèse's eyes widened as if the question was somehow a trap. She asked, bewildered, "To the Americas?"

Alix nodded.

"Yes," answered the maid in a breath.

"Good. Do you have money to bring?"

"No, I send all my salary to my family."

"Any belongings you would like to bring?" Thérèse shook her head. "Alright, then wear my other riding outfit and take some warm clothes whilst I bag the jewels and money."

The two women worked side by side, preparing for their unexpected trip. Soon, they were walking quietly through the corridors of the castle, then the courtyard. They passed the main door and waited outside.

Suddenly, Thérèse made a strangled noise. "Lord Henri found us!"

"It's fine, he is helping us," answered Alix.

Both Thérèse and Henri were startled to see each other. The young man had brought Nettle.

"You are running away with your maid?" he asked incredulously. As Alix did not deign to answer, he sighed and carried on. "I filled the saddles with food. Here is a letter for my friends in New York and here is a map of the area. Avoid people, hide if necessary and," he looked at her, "try to be… more masculine. Hide your hair and wear large clothes, so people think that you are boys."

The two girls nodded; as Alix turned to mount the horse, Henri took her hand. "Be careful," he said softly.

He put his hand on the side of her face, his thumb caressing her cheek. Slowly he bent down and kissed her softly. Thinking that it might be the last time she would see him, Alix put her hands on his torso and felt his heart beating – perhaps as fast as hers. He broke off the kiss and their foreheads touched.

"You did not slap me this time."

She smiled. "Not every time."

He laughed. "I will remember that in the future."

Without giving her time to answer, he took her by the waist and put her on the horse before doing the same to Thérèse.

Alix and Henri looked at each other, serious. "Thank you

for your help," she finally said in a tight voice.

"Follow the road and at the fork, take the left road and keep going up north. The map will help you get to Lorient... May God be with you."

"May God be with you," the two girls answered back.

After a last look, Alix kicked Nettle and the two girls left Beg Hastel.

SIX

September 1688

'Victor' had been on the pirate ship for a few weeks now and she was not sure what to make of it. Contrary to her previous position, she was not there to run the captain's errands. They taught her to navigate the ship on her own; she could now go in the rig as if it was land, keep the helm through a storm and take care of the cannons. She enjoyed exploring the galleon and already felt really attached to it. She particularly loved the figurehead – even though she had never had the opportunity of seeing it in full. It was a mermaid getting ready for war, a sword in one hand and a knife in the other; Vivien was fascinated by her and spent most of her free time on the forecastle looking at it. Overall, the crew liked her, but she could tell that they were not telling her everything. Yet, she also had her secrets and she knew that they felt it; the first mate, One-eyed Harry, kept a close eye on her, seemingly expecting for the girl to betray the crew. She heard him once mumbling that the captain was too good and trusting.

A few weeks after she joined the crew, Vivien had really bad period pain. It did not happen often, but that day, she could barely move out of the hammock. She refused to call the doctor and just accepted a bit of food and water. One of the female crew members, a blonde woman called Daniela, gave her a strange look, but the girl was in too much pain to really pay attention. The following day, she felt much better and resumed her chores. Before lunch time, she was summoned in the captain's cabin on the aft. It had never happened before and Vivien was a bit scared; she checked that her knives were in place and, a bit reassured, she knocked at the door and entered. The captain's stateroom was bigger than she had expected, with large windows at the back offering a breath-taking view of the ocean. The room had a large bed, several chests, shelves with a few books, a desk and a couple of chairs. Sitting in one himself, the captain invited her to sit.

"I have been made aware of your travesty, little girl. Care to explain why you lied to us?"

Vivien's heart skipped a beat. From what she had seen, the captain was not a bad man, but she had seen when she arrived on the ship with Evan that he did not like to be lied to. She answered, her chin bravely out, "No one asked me if I was a boy or a girl. I cannot be considered guilty of your assumptions."

The captain kept on looking at her, his light blue eyes not showing any emotion. Suddenly, he broke out into a smile that radically changed his face, making him less intimidating and scary. "Fair enough. What's your name?"

She hesitated for a second but did not see any reason not to answer. "Vivien, but you can call me Vi."

"How old are you?"

"Sixteen."

"Older than I thought; you are very small."

"I am aware," answered Vivien in an annoyed tone.

The man chuckled before becoming serious again; once the smile left his eyes, Vivien felt a cold chill taking hold of her. This man was powerful and dangerous, and he knew it.

"Why did you want to become a pirate? You are young, you could have a happy future ahead of you if you wanted…"

The girl thought about lying but did not see any benefit in it: he would know if she was lying and she was sure he would not appreciate her lack of honesty.

"Revenge," she answered truthfully. The captain raised an eyebrow, indicating for her to continue. Vivien took a deep breath. "My fiancé was a sailor on a merchant ship. A few months ago they were attacked and killed by pirates; only one of the men survived…"

"The Ghost," asserted the captain in a breath.

Vivien was surprised at his insight but did not comment on it, just nodding in approval. She carried on emphatically. "I enrolled on a ship, came to the Caribbean and managed to become a crew member on a pirate ship," she added with a sly smile. "I vowed to avenge him and I understand it isn't your goal – I wouldn't want to put you and your crew in a bad situation. So if you know any ship led by someone who has anything against the Ghost, I would be more than happy to join that crew."

The captain stood up and went to look out the window. He stayed silent for a long time, looking at the irregular tide, lost in his thoughts. Vivien was getting restless, anxious at knowing his feelings on her story and, perhaps, discover something of interest about her nemesis...

"The Ghost has many enemies," started the man. "As you must have heard, he is heartless, leaving no witnesses and taking all the goods he can." Even though he could not see her, Vivien nodded. "All that I found out is that his ship has no distinctive sign, no figurehead or anything. He mostly attacks ships coming back from the colonies, loaded with sugar, indigo and tobacco. Production has recently started in the Caribbean, but sugar and indigo are in high demand in Europe. It is very difficult to know when the ships are attacked, but it's about every two or three months. You're more than welcome to stay here as I also have some unfinished business with the Ghost."

He fell silent and Vivien was not sure what to do. Would he talk more? Should she leave?

She set up for carrying on the conversation. "What did he do to you?" Her voice was low and unsure; it was abnormal to her and she hated it.

The captain pulled himself from the view and went to open a chest, then took a bottle and two wood glasses. He came back to the desk and put a generous dose of alcohol in each glass. He pushed one towards Vivien before starting to drink his. She smelled the tumbler – rum, she should have expected as much. Taking another long sip, the captain seemed to relax.

"In my youth, I was in the navy; after I retired, I became

a merchant sea captain. Got a wife and a few kids… I had a good life… When he was about your age, my oldest son wanted to follow my steps and became a cabin boy. As he didn't want to be seen as the captain's son, he enrolled on another ship." He looked at her, with sorrow in his eyes. "You can imagine what happened next."

Vivien nodded and murmured, "The Ghost killed him too."

"Aye. At first, I wanted to carry on with my life – you see, my community is very religious and peaceful – but I had so much anger in me, I started to drink and became abusive towards my wife and our younger children. I had already broken the promise I made to God to not be violent, so I decided to do what was best: leave them and find justice for my son. It wasn't easy and neither my wife nor kids understood it at first, but now they see the good we can do, even as pirates."

Vivien was a bit surprised by this ominous statement but was not comfortable enough to push it forward. There was another silence, also broken by Vivien after taking a sip of rum and grimacing.

"How long have you been looking for him?"

He shrugged. "About five years now."

Vivien opened her eyes wide: five years! And he only had a few elements…

"I know it isn't much, but he is a volatile enemy. No one knows who he is, where he is from, where he will attack. His crew doesn't speak out, so no one is connected to him. Why do you think he is called the Ghost? That's not even his ship's name; it's just how this elusive bastard's been nicknamed." The captain finished his rant, slamming the cup on the desk. "We have to board a few more ships before having enough money to buy sustenance and pay the crew's salary for a long trip."

"Are all crew members as… involved as we are?"

"Aye, most of them lost a friend or a family member to the Ghost; just a few of them are attracted by the adventure and the fame that would come from killing the Ghost."

Vivien nodded, taking another small sip of her drink. She wanted to ask about Evan but stopped herself – what difference would it make? She felt the intense look of the captain on her and that made her queasy.

"Something tells me that with a bit more training you'll be a fine addition to our crew."

She raised her eyebrow. "How so?"

"You are hard at work and quick to learn. You have good reflexes and you don't let people walk all over you. I can see you becoming a fierce pirate – well, at least with some training."

Vivien blushed, surprised and happy to receive some praise. Since she had started to hunt for her family, there had been no compliment or positive feedback on anything she had done, and she had to admit, it felt good. She smiled shyly.

Gruffly, the captain scolded her. "Don't get used to it, little girl! Now go back to work."

With a last smile, Vivien jumped to her feet and went back to the bridge.

From that day onward, Vivien became the protégée of the captain. He made sure she learnt how to handle anything on the ship; he taught her how to fight with a knife and a sword, and the best manoeuvres to attack other vessels. Vivien was deeply excited by all this knowledge; she felt more and more at ease on the ship, up until the point that it became her home. Her life in Delaware, her family, everything felt like an old, boring dream and her life on the boat was the real one. She still loved Michael and was eager to avenge him, but her pain and sorrow diminished as her love for the ship and the lifestyle she was living increased. It felt so right. She was afraid at first that the crew would resent her, but the vast majority of them liked her. The most notable exceptions were Bill and Daniela. Why? Vivien did not know, but they both disliked her…

October 1688

Just one more ship to board and they would be ready to go and look for the Ghost. They were, however, not in luck finding their next victim. The last ships they spotted were too fast for them – they probably were empty too. The crew spent most of its days killing time, in the hope that some heavily loaded vessel would come around… And they finally got lucky.

"Ship on the starboard," shouted Jimmy, who was on watch that day.

In a few minutes, everyone was on the bridge to get a look at on the ship. The first mate, One-eyed Harry, took a spyglass and checked it.

"A galleon, seems to be heavy. Well done, Jimmy! Guys, get ready for the collision."

Every pirate grabbed his weapons and went to his post. Cannons were loaded and ready to fire. Vivien, who was near the figurehead, could almost see the instant that the galleon's watchmen saw them. She imagined their fear and panic. They put out their sails, but they were too heavy to properly gain speed; the *Mermaid* was coming at them hard and fast. Soon the two ships were almost parallel; that's when she recognised the figurehead and the name of the ship: *Princess Anne*. Vivien felt dizzy for a second and she knew she could not participate in this boarding. She stayed on the forecastle whilst her crew members went to fight; it was unusual and she noticed the surprised glances the captain, Evan and some others shot her, but, even though she had no loyalty for that crew, she could not hurt them. The fight finished shortly, with several crewmen of both ships harmed; thankfully no one had died. She looked at the bridge of the *Princess Anne*, full of defeated men and blood splatters. Vivien joined the crew on the other ship and went to the captain.

"It's a slave ship," she whispered.

The captain shot her a sharp glance and nodded. "Evan, Bill, go and check the shipment. Daniela, go fetch Pierre."

Both men nodded and went in the hold. The captain then turned to the men on the bridge and asked with an affable voice, "Now, who's in charge here?"

Captain Johnson stood up and answered with a haughty voice, "It is I, pirate."

His bravado made the pirates laugh, especially as his face was white and damp, displaying signs of fear.

"Do you believe in God?" asked the pirate.

Taken aback, the man blinked and became red. "Of course I believe in God!"

Annoyance radiated through his body. Vivien realised that that man she found so impressive when she was his cabin boy, appeared now as a pathetic rooster. He had no authority other than his social position and, compared to the pirates she had lived with the past few months, he was out of shape and somewhat small. Being in the company of pirates had changed her and her vision of the world.

"So you believe in charity, helping the poorest of us?"

"Aye, I often show generosity on land and on sea; you can ask my crew."

The pirate captain nodded. "What about the famous quote of the Gospel of Matthew, when Jesus declares 'the last shall be first and the first last'?"

Johnson shrugged, feeling confident now in the conversation. "Isn't that supposed to only affect the world to come? I believe in it indeed."

The captain nodded, seeing from the corner of his eye Evan and Bill coming from the hold with slaves. "Can you then tell me how you show charity in trading slaves?"

Johnson gasped and looked around just to see a few slaves blinking in the sunlight. Pierre, who had joined them, went to talk to the slaves. As Vivien had discovered, he was a former slave snatched by Frenchmen when he was a child from his village in Africa – he was too young to remember much. After being sold to a surgeon who used him as his assistant, he managed to escape and joined various pirate crews before ending up on the *Mermaid*. His background and expertise gave him a privileged position on the ship as surgeon and translator – he had mastered the language of his tribe, a few others he picked up whilst enslaved, French and English. He also knew how to read, which made him an asset for the crew.

Johnson shrugged and added with contempt, "They don't

need generosity; they are just merchandise. I buy them and sell them, that's all."

It seemed to Vivien that all members of the pirate crew held their breath and looked at the man with disbelief. She glanced at her captain, but he seemed as relaxed and in control of the situation as he had a few minutes ago.

He finally spoke in a cold and calm voice. "Then you don't deserve to live. I am not one to torture, so you will just be sent overboard. You can either jump or we will make you jump."

Johnson had become white in mere seconds, his face flooded with sweat. Vivien felt a pang of pity for him, but then she saw the slaves coming out of the hold one by one, scared, tired and malnourished, and she did not mind seeing that wretched man dying. Johnson stayed immobile for some long seconds, whilst his men looked at the floor, fearful of being next. The captain made a sign and two pirates took the man by the armpits and threw him overboard before he managed to react. The captain then turned to the remaining crew and asked, "Who's the second?"

The man came forward, doing his best not to look frightened. Getting further away by the minute, Vivien could hear the desperate screams of Captain Johnson.

"Me, sir."

The pirate looked at him for some time, memorising his face. "You are in charge of this ship until it gets back to its original harbour. If I find you, your crew or your ship trading humans one more time, you'll all end up like your captain. Am I clear?"

"Aye."

"Good – we are then going to take all your slaves and goods and leave you to it."

The new captain made a step forward. "If you take everything we have, we won't be able to make it to the harbour."

Unmoved, the pirate shot him a hard look. "A bit of hunger is nothing compared to what happen to slaves on a daily basis. Maybe that experience will teach you something…"

Vanquished, the new captain went back in line.

"Vi! Help Pierre bring our guests to the *Mermaid*."

Hearing that name, the crew of the *Princess Anne* looked up and straight at her. She read successively surprise, anger and hate on their face. It scared her a bit, but she did not care: these people were not good; she was better off with the pirates than them…

A couple of days later, they arrived near land by a succession of islands. Vivien was at her usual post, near the figurehead looking at the beautiful scenery. She felt a presence and saw Evan near her.

"What's this?"

He squinted, smiling broadly. "Hello to you too, lovely lady."

She shook her head, not in the mood for the man's flirty banter. He was as much a thief as a flirt, and he had added her to his list of females to dally with as soon as he had discovered her gender. Even though she kept telling him off, he did not stop, which annoyed her even more.

"Evan, you are aggravating me again."

He shrugged, his eyes glowing in the sunny morning. "It's part of my charm."

She snorted. "It certainly isn't!" She shook her head. "Anyway, what's this place?"

"We've arrived at the mouth of the Cape Fear River. There are a few places on these islands that are ideal for people like us to hide, amongst other things."

Vivien nodded. "I see. What are the other things?"

Evan had a mischievous smile. "You will learn soon enough!"

She sighed, exasperated, while he went back to work.

That afternoon, the captain knowingly steered the ship in between small islands until they followed a river. The place was ideal for pirates in between the land and the islands, with the sandbanks, the numerous coves and the luxurious vegetation. Vivien avidly looked around, admiring the wild landscape; she also wondered what they were doing here, as there were no traces of humans. When they came to a halt, anchoring the ship before the river became too narrow, her puzzlement deepened. Yet, soon she noticed some movement on the coastline; at the same time, the pirates were bringing down the rowboats, bringing small groups of slaves on shore. It took a long time and Vivien was too far away to see what was happening. Finally, she was on the last boat to go to land; it had been weeks since she had been on the boat and walking on steady ground felt very strange to her. She followed the group and, after a short walk, they arrived at a small village, well hidden by the vegetation. There were dozens of small and sturdy wood houses, and what appeared to be around fifty inhabitants. They were built around two roads crossing in the middle where there was a house, a small square and a well. There was enough space on each side to build more lodgings

ANN PARKER

if necessary. Vivien saw a couple of crew members go to hug some of the people – friends or family members, she assumed.

She spotted Evan not far from her and went to him. "What's happening here?"

Smiling broadly, he put his arm around her shoulders; she tensed but did not push him back. "Freedom."

Puzzled, she looked up to him, cursing her short stature. "How so?"

"When we board a slave ship, we bring the people here. It's a small village built by some Quakers," he indicated the captain talking with a middle-aged woman and a couple of kids around the same age as Vivien, "including the captain's family. They are against slavery, so we bring them the people we rescue and they help them acclimate to the colonies, learn the language and offer them freedom. They can stay around or go in some cities up north like Baltimore or Philadelphia, or, in the south, the new town of Charlestown."

Vivien was drinking in his words – she was bewildered and strangely happy about the existence of this village and these good people. Once more she was convinced that she had made a good choice in joining those pirates: not only had they given her freedom and the opportunity to avenge Michael but they were quite good people. The thought of Captain Johnson and his death came to her mind, but she shoved it away; she was not sure he had deserved to die, but he certainly was not a good man by her book.

"Do you often come here?"

Evan shrugged. "A couple of times per year, mostly for the crew to see friends and family. I think we got a couple of slave

113

ships over the past years, not more, so we brought them here too. We prefer money anyway."

Vivien side-glanced at him and saw that he had his usual cocky smile. She was not sure whether he was joking and did not ask.

"What are the Quakers?" She had never heard of them before and was quite intrigued.

Evan was surprised by her question and seemed to remember that he was talking to a young girl without much experience and knowledge of life – always flirting and joking, he had forgotten that… Even if Vivien did not understand why, she saw a shift in his features and the way he looked at her and it annoyed her.

After a short silence, Evan answered, "I don't know much about them – mostly that they value people equally and are against violence." Vivien shot him an astonished glance and Evan nodded. "I know, being pirates definitively doesn't fit with being a Quaker… That's probably why the captain is more a pirate nowadays!"

The girl thought of the talk she had had with the captain in his cabin some time ago, and his enigmatic words made sense now. "I would like to know more about these Quakers – they seem to be good people," she muttered.

Evan nodded. "They are," he acquiesced, serious for once, but it did not last. "Oh well, for the time that we are on shore, I hope there aren't only Quaker girls here – they are no fun!"

A bit scandalised, Vivien could not help but smile. That was the thing with Evan: his good spirit was always contagious, even when he was making unladylike comments. She decided to tease him, playing the innocent and naïve girl.

"But I thought that your intentions towards Daniela were pretty serious and that there would be a marriage to celebrate soon. That would be so lovely! Can you imagine, both of you in your best attire, all of us on the bridge and the captain marrying you?"

During her short speech, Evan had become a bit green and kept on glancing around to find Daniela, either to confront her or to flee. It became really hard for Vivien to keep a straight face and, as soon as her smile became more playful, Evan eyed her suspiciously. "Are you playing me, little girl?"

Repressing a giggle, Vivien answered in the most serious way she could: "Certainly not, sir, I am but an honest and kind maiden."

At that point she could not stop herself from laughing and, good sport that he was, so did Evan. "You tricked me, little minx! I appreciate your attempt, but I will get my revenge."

His words might have been threatening, but his smile recanted them. She smiled too and they stayed looking at each other in pleasant silent for some time, until a voice called her. Feeling her cheeks grow hot for no reason, she shook her head and went to see the captain.

"Charlotte, please meet Vivien, our newest recruit," said the captain in a formal tone. "Vivien, my wife, Charlotte."

She was a woman in her forties with a pleasant face, currently torn by an unhappy smile. Her eyes were brown and her greying hair used to be blonde. Her clothes were very simple, more than what Vivien used to wear back home and did not flatter her figure, but she did not care – that was plain.

"Pleased to meet you," said the girl with a smile.

Charlotte nodded and asked in a reproving tone,

"Same… though, what brings such a young girl to embark on a pirate ship?"

Vivien looked at her in silence, cocking her head. "Injustice, ma'am – my fiancé was murdered; I won't find solace until his killer is in Hell."

The captain did not expect her to use such strong language, and neither did she, but she could not stop it. She had done nothing wrong and was not going to take any kind of judgement from anyone.

Shocked, Charlotte replied, "What terrible language, young lady, and terrible ideas too! You should cherish human life, not want to destroy it."

Before the captain could interrupt, Vivien replied, "I do not know your beliefs as a Quaker, but I respect them and I respect you, ma'am. I would appreciate the same kind of respect from you. I might be young, but I have seen enough of the world to know what is right and wrong, and I agree, murder is wrong. Yet, the man I seek to kill has murdered my fiancé, your son and countless others; he clearly does not care about human life. I understand that you might disagree, but in my book, removing that man from earth will be a blessing for all the men and maybe women and children who will never meet him and perish from his blade. Wouldn't you agree?"

She looked both at Charlotte and the captain; the former was bewildered and annoyed, while the latter gazed at her in awe and nodded.

"Aye, this is true and the essence of what I want to do." He took his wife's hands in his. "My dear Charlotte, I know you disagree, and if the circumstances were different,

I probably would, but I cannot bear the idea of that man walking, eating, sleeping and maybe spending time with his loved ones, when he took so much from us and others. He needs to be stopped."

Charlotte brusquely removed her hands and pinched her lips. In a hushed tone, she replied, "I don't completely disagree with the core of what you say, but you don't have to do it yourself!"

The captain looked at her with sadness in his eyes. "You know I can't stay here and do nothing… Also, no one else seems to be willing to do the job."

With a move of her chin, Charlotte indicated Vivien. "She is more than willing to lead the crusade!"

Scandalised, he regarded his wife as if he did not know her. "So you want me to leave a young girl in charge of finding and defeating a dangerous murderer while I stay here?" He shook his head. "I can't do that. I can't leave Vivien to fight alone."

Charlotte pinched her lips. "Just so you know, at the next meeting, I will request to be granted a divorce. I cannot keep on living like this." She observed her husband for a couple of minutes, waiting for a reaction; she found none and left with a strange expression on her face, a mix of sadness and anger.

"Please forgive her – she means well, but her beliefs stop her from accepting our choices."

Vivien nodded and asked, "What beliefs?"

The captain hesitated before answering, "Let's have a walk. My wife and I – actually, the vast majority of people living here are Quakers. Do you know what this is?" Vivien shook her head. "We are Christians, but our values are different from the Catholic or Protestant churches. We believe that God is everywhere and in everybody; we are non-violent and against anything that can harm other human beings, particularly slavery. Because God is everywhere and in everyone, we don't need priests or churches to be close to Him. We also believe in strong community ties and simple life – that's why this community settled here. There is no one around, so they can be autonomous and live by their own rules."

"Like pirates?"

The captain laughed. "Yes, like pirates. The main difference being that we live violently…"

Vivien nodded. "What happens when a crime is committed?"

"We believe in honesty and non-violence. There aren't many crimes in Quaker communities as we live in harmony and behold the same values. The few crimes that have ever happened in the community have been minor ones and didn't need any punishment other than self-reflection."

Vivien hesitated and then asked, "Do you regret leaving your community?" She did not say 'and your family', but it hung in the air.

The captain looked sad for a few seconds before shaking his head. "Nay. I would have betrayed my faith if I had stayed with them."

As they arrived at the edge of some woodland, Vivien frowned. "What do you mean?"

"We Quakers try to live in honesty, honesty to God but also to ourselves. I couldn't live with myself if I had decided not to do anything, to stay put and die without having the Ghost taken care of. I prayed a lot and I realised that I would rather have some blood on my hands than let that evil roam the world."

Vivien nodded – her circumstances were different, but she felt the same.

The captain looked back at the square. "Let's go back, it's almost dinner time!"

They stayed in the village for a few days, helping the former slaves to settle, either joining some households, using the unoccupied houses or building more for them to live in. The pirates also gave them some seeds they had bought for them and the small cattle found on the ship they had boarded. When they weighted the anchor, Vivien knew that soon they would find the Ghost and they would have their revenge.

SEVEN

July 1691

The wind was good and the ship was sailing fast. Alix was surprised at how quickly she had accommodated to life on board. She spent most of her time on the bridge, listening to people and watching the horizon. She had loved the sight of the ocean as soon as she had seen it at Beg Hastel, but now she felt a sort of connection to it. The journey had been going smoothly so far, but something told her that she would also love a storm. Poor Thérèse was not that lucky; she had been suffering from nausea since the first day and was bed-ridden… Soon after they had embarked, she had found out that she was pregnant, which had increased her sea sickness. She was pale and thin, and could not stop crying. Even though Alix was doing everything she could to help her friend, the stuffy and stinky atmosphere of the cabin drew her out. With another couple, they were the only passengers on the ship – the *Marie-Thérèse* mostly transported goods but had a couple of cabins to allow wealthy people to go to the Americas.

Earlier that day, Alix had talked to Captain Morin and learnt that they only had a week before arriving in New York. She felt both happy and anxious about that: she had Henri's letter and believed that she would find refuge there, but she had a nagging feeling that something would happen and change her plans. *Also it's not as if I've had good experiences with travels and expectations!* She scolded herself, using her free time to think of other options: after all, Thérèse and her had money and jewels hidden in their clothes; they could survive… If they sold everything, they could buy a small house, but how would they earn money? She could become a private teacher, but would she have a good enough salary? Perhaps it would be best to open a shop? Or a private school? At least that way they would be able to survive on their own. Alix quite liked this idea; it was better than living off of Henri's friends' charity.

Alix must have dozed off, as some shouts and running around woke her up. One of the sailors passed by her, urging her to get back to her cabin. Curious, she looked around to see what was happening and that's when she saw it: several metres away on the starboard side, a galleon was coming at them hard and fast. The ship was majestic and its figurehead – an armed mermaid – was both beautiful and terrifying, but what was more chilling was the black and white pirate flag. Even though it was still quite far away, Alix could see pirates getting ready to board the ship, and a kind of terror she had never known washed over her. She managed to tear her gaze away from the enemy ship, yet she was too frightened to think clearly and go back to her cabin, so she moved back to a corner and tried to hide.

On the *Mermaid*, Vivien was getting ready for the boarding. A lot had changed since she had joined the crew: she had improved her skills and was able to work at every station on the ship; the captain had also insisted on teaching her how to properly fight and she had now daily training sessions with him or Evan; her good relationship with the crew had only increased – still with the exception of Bill and Daniela, for reasons she did not understand. On the downside, they had not found the *Ghost* yet, nor any lead as to where he could be. They recently had resorted to letting everyone know that the captain of the *Mermaid* was looking for him. Vivien was not sure it was the best strategy, but the captain was adamant that, at this point, it was their only option.

She shook her head, chasing away unwanted thoughts. *It is neither the time nor the place to think of that.* She looked up at the ship in front of them: French flag, smaller than them and obviously heavy with its shipment, it was going to be a good haul. Vivien smiled, enjoying the anticipation of the fight and the run-up to victory. Soon they were on the ship; the manoeuvre to make the *Mermaid* parallel to the other went smoothly, as usual. They threw their grappling hooks and lines to keep the two ships close during the boarding. Without wasting time, Vivien signalled for the pirates to attack. The men on the other ship tried to fight back, but it was not enough, and in about fifteen minutes, the pirates had gained full control. The captain arrived on the bridge with Pierre and gave orders for the *Marie-Thérèse* to be searched; the surgeon was there to translate when necessary. It was a good haul: mostly expensive fineries and delicately ornamented furniture.

"Look what I found! A little mouse hiding," shouted Bill from the side; as usual, he was drunk. Vivien even wondered where he managed to hide his stash of alcohol.

Vivien turned and saw the sailor holding a girl by the arm. She was obviously scared, her blue eyes almost popping out of her head. She clearly made an effort to regain composure and stood straight in front of the curious gaze of the pirates.

"Can I have my fun with the mouse?" he asked greedily.

Vivien was shocked; even though they were pirates, such a situation had never happened since she had joined the crew and her dislike for the man instantly turned to utter disgust and hate.

She growled, "Certainly not!"

He grunted, still holding the girl. She was young and her fear made her look even younger. His grip must have been strong as she grimaced every time he moved.

"I'm not asking you, Victor. You clearly lack the balls to get her!" He laughed at his own joke.

Vivien was reassured that none of the men joined him; even if no one of them said anything, some shifted uneasily.

"Still, the answer is no. We take their merchandise; we don't injure people for no bloody reason."

"There is a reason…" he answered, groping his groin.

Seeing him distracted, the girl broke free and grabbed his sword before shouting, "*Ne vous approchez pas de moi!*[1]"

---

1   Do not come near me.

Bill swore, put out a knife and went to her. The girl looked frightened, but her grip on the sword was tight. The pirates did not intervene – her inexperience was balanced by Bill's drunkenness. She checked that there was nothing to block her and took a step back, Bill inexorably walking towards her. He launched, but she jumped on her right side, the sword cutting the air. He fell forward, ending up kneeling. Bill got up, more furious than before.

"Fucking blowsabella! I'll end you!"

The girl peeked at the other pirates, who were silently watching the scene. She was clearly terrorised. Bill used her distraction to launch his attack and fell on her. They both shouted in pain and stopped moving, the bloody sword pointing straight towards the sky. Vivien signalled to two men to untangle the bodies: the sword was deep in Bill's belly and blood was flooding. He was still alive and whining, but the girl was out, the knife on her side.

Pierre came forward to examine them. "Nothing to do for him. She can survive, though – the blade went almost straight in and likely did not touch any major organ. A few stitches and she should be fine."

The captain, who was supervising the moving of the shipment, arrived then. "What's happening?"

"Bill was drunk and attacked the girl. He is dying and she is hurt. Pierre needs to stitch her up."

The captain looked at the scene, weighing up his options. The girl was unconscious on the floor, her messy light hair around her pale face and her clothes soaked with blood.

"Let's show Bill some mercy and end his suffering. The girl can come with us."

Vivien turned towards him, taken aback. "You mean, on the ship with us?"

The captain looked at her, his face devoid of any expression. "Are you questioning my orders?" he snapped.

Vivien took a step back, intimidated by his tone and the cold shine of his light blue eyes. She shook her head. "Of course not, it is just unorthodox."

The captain shrugged and answered, with a smile, "We are pirates – everything we do is unorthodox."

Vivien nodded and Evan took the girl in his arms to bring her on the *Mermaid*. At the same time, a shout erupted a bit further away and a woman arrived, shouting and crying. "*Ne la touchez pas! Laissez-la!²*"

She came towards them and was going to hit Evan, but Pierre stopped her and held her in his arms. She was also young, with brown hair and eyes, and she would have been pretty if her skin had not been waxy and her eyes hollow; and pregnant.

Being held made her even more frantic. "*Lâchez-moi, je vous interdit de me toucher!³*"

As the pirates were looking at the scene with confusion, Pierre translated. "She wants me to let her go and you," he indicated Evan, "to let this one go."

The captain intervened. "Talk to her."

Pierre nodded. "*Mademoiselle, je vais vous lâcher, mais vous devez vous calmer.⁴*"

She stopped struggling and he let her go.

---

2   Do not touch her! Leave her be!

3   Leave me alone, I forbid you to touch me.

4   Miss, I will let you go, but you must calm down.

"*Laissez-là aussi,*⁵" she demanded.

Pierre shook his head. "*Elle est blessée et a besoin de soins.*⁶"

The woman pinched her lips, unconvinced. "*Ils peuvent le faire ici.*⁷"

Once more, Pierre shook his head. "*Je ne pense pas qu'ils aient un chirurgien.*" He turned towards the kneeling sailors. "*Y a-t-il un docteur sur ce bâteau pour aider la jeune fille blessée?*⁸"

All of them shook their heads.

"*Il n'y a pas d'autre choix…*⁹"

She straightened her spine and raised her chin. "*Dans ce cas, je viens avec vous. Il s'agit de ma soeur et je ne vais pas l'abandonner. Je vais chercher nos affaires.*¹⁰" The girl darted into the ship.

Intrigued, the captain looked at Pierre. "So?"

"She wants to come with us – apparently they are sisters."

The captain nodded. "It's probably for the best." As Vivien gasped on his side, he added, "They don't know the colonies; we all know it is a hard life, even more when you are alone and pregnant.

Vivien wanted to object, but he was right: leaving that girl alone was almost condemning her… She nodded. When the girl came back with a couple of small bags – which made

---

5 Let her go.
6 She is injured and need help.
7 They can do it here.
8 I don't think they have a surgeon. Is there a doctor on this ship to treat the injured girl?
9 There is no other choice.
10 In this case, I am coming with you. We are sisters and I will not abandon her. I will fetch our belongings.

Vivien wonder who these women were to travel with so little – Pierre helped her go to the *Mermaid*. The last bit of shipment taken, the pirates removed the grappling hooks and line and set sail to go far away from the French ship.

It had been two days and Alix was feverish. She would wake up, eat and drink a bit, and then go back to an unrestful sleep full of nightmares and pain. Seeing Thérèse every time she opened her eyes soothed her.

Three more days and Alix woke up with a weak body but a clear mind. Her left side was painful – she remembered the attack – but she felt better. Thérèse was not in the cabin, so she sat on the small bed, looking around for water. She would not say no to some food either, as her grumbling stomach reminded her. She put her feet on the floor and cautiously walked to the pitcher of water.

As she was drinking, Thérèse came into the room and let out a cry of joy. "Alix, you are awake!" She came to her and hugged her. "I am so relieved to see you moving."

Alix hugged her back and observed her. Her friend looked healthier, with rounder cheeks and clear skin. "You look good too!"

Thérèse smiled and blushed. "Pierre – I mean, the doctor gave me some herbs to help with the nausea and I feel so much better."

Alix took her hands. "I am happy for you." She paused and came closer to speak. "Thérèse, what's happening?"

The girl fidgeted a bit before answering. "You remember the pirates attacking us?" Alix nodded. "Well, you were hurt and they took us with them."

Alix became white; she went to one of the windows but only could see the endless ocean. She felt dizzy and went back to sit on the bed. Understanding that her friend did not feel good, Thérèse left the cabin to look for Pierre. A few minutes after, he entered, finding Alix deep in her thoughts.

"You have awakened – that's a very good sight to see. How do you feel?"

She started and looked up to the man speaking her language with a slight accent. Never before she had seen a black man, so she was both surprised and wary. As she did not answer, he added with a smile, "I am the surgeon on this ship, but please call me Pierre."

Alix glanced at Thérèse, who was clearly at ease with the man, watching him with admiration in her eyes. *Or maybe more*, wondered Alix. She relaxed a bit. "My name is Alix and I am fine."

He nodded. "Good, you have been stabbed and had a fever afterwards, so you did not eat or drink properly. You will feel weak for a few days, so eat well and don't overdo it."

"Can I speak to the captain?"

If he was surprised, Pierre did not show it. "I am the only one who can speak French on this ship. What do you need?"

She pinched her lips, annoyed. She remembered now that the man who had grabbed her spoke another language, but she had hoped he would be the only one.

"Where are we going? When will you be releasing us?"

He stayed silent for some time, glancing at Thérèse, unsure how to phrase it. "There is no plan to release you currently as we are not sailing to any commercial harbour where you would be safe," he started cautiously. "You'll have to stay on board until then, I am afraid."

Alix opened her mouth to object, but Thérèse had rushed to her side and hugged her. "We don't have any choice," she whispered in her ear. "I don't think they'll hurt us, so let's see where it goes and make the most of it."

Unconvinced, Alix stared at her before nodding. *It's not as if we have any other choice anyway...*

December 1691

After months of sailing around, attacking ships and selling their loot in shady harbours, the pirates had come to visit a small village in a place called Carolina. It was poor and simple and, as the captain told them, a place where people of all colour and gender were free and equal. If she had not been living on a pirate ship for the past five months, Alix would have probably never believed it, but so much had changed. It was hard to adjust to their new situation – more for her than for Thérèse, who quickly created a close bond with Pierre. She was afraid all the time, both because of the assault, and the fact that they were pirates, and, therefore in her mind, bad people. Yet, after a few weeks, she realised that life was not black or white, and that it was the same for pirates. No one attacked them or belittled them; they had chores like everyone else.

Every morning, Pierre taught English to Thérèse and Alix, and without having any other option to communicate with people, they managed to learn the basics of the language quite quickly. It did not mean that Alix became friends with anyone – she had learnt that they did not want to hurt her, but it did not mean that she trusted them, and the feeling was mutual. She could see that now that she understood English, they were wary of what they said around her. Vivien – the captain's protégée – disliked her, particularly since the captain had become interested in Alix and called her into his cabin almost every day to talk. Vivien felt as if he was slowly replacing her with the other girl, educated, beautiful and impressionable. He was particularly interested in knowing more about Jansenism; he enjoyed telling her about his own faith and starting debates on almost every topic. Week after week, Alix had come to appreciate and respect him; sometimes she even wished her father would have been more like him – kind, open to discussion, driven by anything else other than faith and money...

By Christmas, Thérèse was heavily pregnant; she was not sure when she would give birth, but it would probably be in the following days or week. Her feet were swollen, her back ached and she could barely sleep. No one said anything, but she knew she was a burden on the crew. She was then relieved when they arrived in the village. Some pirates went to their families, whilst the rest settled in a large house intended to host travellers. Pierre told them about the village, so they were not surprised to see so many black people mingling with whites and dealing with them as equals. It made both girls wonder about their position in life: Thérèse was raised believing that she was worth less than nobility and even wealthy people, whilst Alix had grown up believing that she was in the middle and, therefore, that her life was worth more than most. Yet, those people, the Quakers, showed them that hierarchy was not necessary to make society work and thrive. The weather was cold; it was even snowing, which neither her nor Alix had seen much in France. They both watched snowflakes pouring from the sky with fascination. Vivien stayed with the captain and his family, whilst the girls were meant to share a room in the large house.

On Christmas Eve, they had barely started eating when Thérèse felt something wet. They were invited in the captain's family home and, mortified, she thought she had peed herself until the captain's wife – or ex-wife; she was a bit confused – told her that her water had broken. The birth was long and exhausting, the baby only arriving the day after around midday – a son. Alix spent the night and the morning outside of the room, anxiously waiting for the delivery – she had to be honest, anxiously waiting for Thérèse to pass this ordeal and survive. It was not that she did not care about the baby, but her friend had been there for her like no other person in her life – with the exception of Henri – and she did not know what she would do if anything happened to her. Finally, Pierre called her into the room to take the screaming baby. Thérèse was on the bed, pale and sweaty.

Clearly still in pain, she managed a smile towards Alix and said in a low voice, "Take care of him – you are his godmother."

Holding back her tears, Alix nodded, forcing a smile on her face. She stepped forward to get to Thérèse and hold her hand, but Pierre pushed her out. After one last look at his worried face, she closed the door and took the screaming baby into the sitting room.

Trying to calm him down, she observed his face and sighed, mumbling absentmindedly, "You look like just your father…"

Alix had not noticed Vivien and the captain sitting on the other side of the room. She stiffened when she heard the other girl asking, "It doesn't seem to make you happy…" Alix turned, holding the baby closer. Vivien cocked her head and added, "Let me guess, you were in love with the guy but he preferred your sister?"

"Vi," growled the captain as a warning.

Alix could not help the disgusted expression that came to her face, which attracted the attention of the two others. They exchanged a curious look and she knew that the captain wanted to know now. She tried to deflect, using her own worry for her friend. "Do you think Thérèse will be OK? Pierre is still inside…"

Vivien shrugged and the captain answered in a soothing voice, "He will do his best. Thérèse is strong and young – she will survive."

Alix nodded, a few tears streaming down her face, but she knew it was just wishful thinking. She should be praying for Thérèse's life, but she had to take care of the child of a man she despised. Yet it was her friend's wish and she would do anything to honour the implicit promise she had made a few minutes prior; he was the child of Thérèse and she would do anything in her power to ensure that this baby would never become the same kind of man his father was.

They stayed in silence for some time, until Vivien asked again, "So who's the father?"

Annoyed, Alix answered bluntly, "My fiancé."

Her declaration was met with silence until the captain whistled. "That's a turn of events…"

"And not only do you talk to your sister but you'll take care of her child too?" enquired a bewildered Vivien.

Alix shook her head and started to rock the baby, who was whining. She sighed but felt it was time for them to know the truth about her. "Thérèse isn't my sister, she is my maid, and what my fiancé did to her was her reason for leaving. As for me, his family intended to kill me soon after the marriage, so I didn't feel like staying and waiting for the hatchet."

Vivien and the captain remained silent for a long time, until he asked, "Where were you going?"

Not seeing any reason to hide the rest of the story, Alix carried on. "New York. Henri, my fiancé's brother, helped us leave and had friends there who could hide us—"

Vivien interjected, "You're coming from France, right?" Alix nodded. "Why not go to your family?"

"That was my first instinct, but Henri told us that his family would look there first, so we would not be able to arrive there safely."

"Why not stay in another city or a village? Surely these people cannot search every single house in the kingdom!"

"Henri said that New York was safer, that his friends would help us and that he would come for us…"

Saying it, Alix realised how foolish she had been, not only in trusting him but also in doing everything he said. She looked at Vivien and she could see that the woman had very similar thoughts, but to her credit, she did not say anything. Her words hung in the air, no one knowing how to change the topic. She stood up, walking while cradling the baby – without any luck. Never having been in the presence of young children, much less new-borns, Alix was not sure what to do.

"I think he might be hungry," suggested the captain.

The girl shot an anxious look at the door separating them from Thérèse. "I don't think she is able to do anything for him now…" Her voice broke, but she held back her tears.

"I'll go look if there is another young mother in the village who could breastfeed him," said the captain before leaving the room.

Alix and Vivien looked awkwardly at each other, not sure what to say. There was still a rampant animosity between them, an untold jealousy, but at that time, it appeared futile to both of them.

"Do you want me to hold him?"

Alix looked at the girl, clearly not expecting this olive branch, but she looked sincere. Alix relaxed and nodded, transferring the whining baby to Vivien. "Thanks, he isn't that heavy, but…"

Vivien nodded. "We should find him a crib, so he'll be able to sleep."

Alix realised that, though they had known about the pregnancy, neither she nor Thérèse had prepared anything. This baby was coming to a world that had not planned for him, almost did not want him. She had never talked with Thérèse about him, but she knew that when she had realised that she was pregnant, she had cried for several days. They were already on the ship and her nausea was keeping her too busy to dwell on the future; even when they had joined the pirate crew and her belly had grown, the existence of the baby had seemed far away, almost not happening. They had so much to do, to learn, that it felt like they had not had the time to prepare and plan for the baby. Facing the harsh reality, Alix realised that they had been careless. And now he was here, without a crib, without clothes, *maybe even without a mother*. Alix's dark thoughts were interrupted by the return of the captain with a black woman a bit older than her. She was dressed simply, as all the Quakers did, and nodded to the two girls.

"This is Maya," said the captain. "She had a little boy not long ago and is willing to feed… the baby until Thérèse feels better."

Alix looked at the wailing child in her arms and felt strangely protective, but if the captain trusted the woman, she was willing to do the same. Maya came forward, her arms opened and Alix placed the child in her arms.

"What a cute baby! What's his name?" asked Maya with a smile.

Alix cursed herself for not even thinking of that; she also knew that he must be baptised at once to ensure that if the worst happened, his soul would go to heaven. She glanced at the corridor, at the end of which laid Thérèse, and she shook her head; she would not name the baby without Thérèse.

"His mum will decide it when she gets better."

Maya gave her a look of pity but nodded in return. "Alright, then I'll start feeding him – he looks like he is starving." She observed him for a few seconds before adding, "He'll also need some clothes very soon." Alix blushed, Maya's words echoing her thoughts and making her feel ashamed. "Don't worry about that – the women in the village have enough old baby clothes for you. If you want, I can take the baby into my home so I'll be around when he needs his next feeding."

Fighting back tears, Alix nodded and thanked the woman with a smile. Once the door closed again, she sat, bereft of any purpose, and waited for news of her friend.

It was late at night when Pierre woke her up. Vivien and the captain had gone to bed already, but Alix had not moved from the sitting room, dozing on the table at some point. She looked at the surgeon with hope, but the look on his face said it all. She felt her breathing stop and something crushed her heart; this could not happen.

"What...?"

"She's lost a lot of blood and is feverish. I did everything I could, but I have reached the limits of my knowledge. I'm sorry."

Alix stood up, her legs numb, but she did not care. Without a word, she put a hand on Pierre's arm and slowly went to the room. The light was weak and the smell of blood overpowering – *the smell of death*. Thérèse was lying on the bed, her drained face strangely relaxed; forming a long braid, her hair was sweaty. Pierre had put a blanket on her and the bed, probably to hide the blood-soaked sheets. Alix took a chair and sat near the bed, taking Thérèse's right hand in hers – it was cold and motionless, yet she could still see her chest slowly rising.

"Thérèse, I'm so sorry for everything. I should have done something to help you, to stop him, then maybe all this would have been avoided." She kissed her hand. "Failing you will always be my biggest regret, but I'll do everything I can for your son. I promise you, I'll take care of him, ensure his safety and that he'll become a good man. You've been a good friend, the best I ever had, and I'll always be grateful to have known you."

Thérèse did not answer and the two girls stayed like that all night. Alix occasionally spoke, more for herself than for

Thérèse, always without response. Soon after dawn broke, Pierre came back to check on the patient – he clearly had barely slept, still in the same clothes and his eyes bloodshot. He searched for a pulse but did not find any. "Alix, I'm sorry, she is gone."

The girl looked at him with empty eyes and did not move, still holding her friend's hand in hers.

The following couple of days remained blurry in Alix's mind. She knew what had happened but did not properly remembered it. They forced her to go to sleep whilst they cleaned Thérèse and the room; they forced her to eat and drink. When she woke up that evening, her friend was resting on the bed, dressed and groomed. For a second, Alix thought that she was sleeping; she looked peaceful, almost happy. She took her place on the side of the bed and remained there the whole night, people coming and going to pay their respects to Thérèse. She could hear their muffled voices in the sitting room but could not make out the words. Some of them put a comforting hand on her shoulder; she never turned around to see who – she did not really care.

They came to pick up Thérèse in the morning. Every inhabitant of the village was gathered around the small cemetery; most of them did not know the deceased, but they all wanted to pay their respects. When Maya arrived, she gave the baby to Alix, who felt strangely better having the newborn in her arms. He was sleeping peacefully, unaware of the tragedy that had already befallen him. One of the oldest men of the village talked for some time – probably about God, but Alix could not remember – then the captain made Thérèse's eulogy and, even though she had barely heard a word, Alix started to cry again. The small ceremony ended soon after, but she stayed there, looking at the hole containing her friend's body and the earth being rhythmically shoved to hide it.

Long after that, the captain came to her and took her arm. "It's time to baptise the baby."

Alix nodded – not only was she was too tired to argue but she also knew that he was right; she had made a promise and she intended to fulfil it.

The same old man celebrated the ceremony with Alix as godmother; she looked around and took Pierre's hand. "You should be the godfather."

Obviously moved, he shook his head. "But I didn't save her," he murmured.

She smiled sadly, rocking the baby. "You did your hardest; it means something."

Tears in his eyes, he nodded and took his place beside her.

"What's the baby's name?" asked the man.

Alix briefly panicked, realising that she had not though of that.

"Peter Henry de Kerhoët."

They all looked strangely at her but did not say anything. A part of her had died with Thérèse, yet she had now a mission: take care of Peter and find a way, one day, to have Louis pay for what he had done to Thérèse. Like almost everyone on the *Mermaid*, she now had someone to avenge.

EIGHT

May 1695

The years had passed, but neither Alix, Vivien nor the captain tasted the sweet flavour of revenge. They had been roaming the American coast up to the Caribbean with no result. Often they would hear about the Ghost's misdeeds, but they were never at the right place to catch him. They were busy, though, boarding ships, taking their wealth and slaves. At least twice a year they went to the village, now known as Hope, just to see their families and friends – however, they caught so many slave ships that they had to come more often. Hope grew; many former slaves left the town, but even more stayed in the community. More Quakers also came, relieved to find some safe haven where they could live in peace.

Even though it broke her heart to leave, Alix had made the choice to remain on the pirate crew and asked if Maya

139

could take care of the child. It was not an easy decision to make, but she had to avenge Thérèse before she could build her life with Peter. She could have gone to France already, but she needed to have a plan and she had not managed yet to find a good one. She still had the letter Henri gave her years ago, but it was stored in a box with some memories; she was aware that they belonged to another person, a naïve and helpless girl, someone she was not anymore. Aged three and a half years, Peter was a lively child, the spitting image of his father, but he had his mother's eyes; every time they saw each other, he reminded Alix who and what she was fighting for. She might have missed a lot of his early days, but she still loved him with all her heart and was never happier than when he called her 'mum'.

On the ship, things had also changed; their proximity to the captain and their abilities led Vivien and Alix to have important positions in the crew. Vivien had become the quartermaster: she distributed rations, powder, work, prizes and punishments. Even though One-eyed Harry was still the first mate, it was obvious to anyone that she was practically the second in command. As for Alix, she had developed an interest in reading and correcting charts, and using navigational tools, so she became the navigator, also known as the sea artist, and the second mate in the chain of command.

Since Thérèse's death, they had became closer. The original animosity Vivien felt for the other girl vanished and she buried a hatchet that was never really dug up. The captain put her in charge of Alix's training, which allowed the girls to bond even more. Vivien was still a bit jealous of her education and literacy, but she had learnt that the captain valued both of them for who they were and their own abilities – and she was a much better huntress than Alix. Their physical proximity led to an emotional relationship and, in about a year, they went from enemies to sisters. They knew everything about each other and were able to interpret each other's behaviour – for instance, Alix knew what the awkward glances that Vivien sometimes shot at Evan meant. They also were close enough that she could tease her, to Vivien's dismay.

One of fair skin and hair, the other one of dark skin and hair; one tall and one small; one shy and one cocky. Described in a book, the two girls could not have been more different, but seeing them together, they appeared similar. Practical clothes, long hair braided, but most importantly, something wild in their eyes, their way of looking at their interlocutors as if they could see straight into their souls. Evan started using their nickname: one day they were talking by the figurehead when he joked that there were now two live mermaids on the ship. The crew soon adopted it, then the inhabitants of Hope and, in the end, the other pirates.

They arrived at the harbour of Port Royal in Jamaica, an English flag flying. A former safe haven for pirates, the city had passed anti-piracy laws a few years prior, making it a risky place. It also meant that it was the perfect town to find information on the Ghost. The flourishing marketplace allowed them to sell their latest loot (exotic spices and woods) for a good price. On the first day, Vivien and the captain went to gather information on the Ghost, his ship or his crew in most taverns in town. They left at the end of the afternoon and came back in the middle of the night. They talked to dozens of people, even administrators of the crown and members of the navy, but did not gather any valuable information and went to bed disgruntled.

On the day after, Vivien went with Evan to the marketplace to buy some necessities and changed her mind. Even though she did not say anything, she was confident they would find information on the Ghost – anything would have given her hope. It had been seven years already since Michael had been killed and, even if the pain had receded, she still needed more to move on. Not finding any lead on where to find the Ghost and his identity was taking its toll on her. She felt a new kind of desperation creeping in and she had to make herself busy in order to keep it at bay. Though he was hiding it better, the captain was in a similar state and spent his days in his cabin, slowly sipping rum and watching the harbour.

In the early evening, a man came, left a message for the captain and dashed off. A few minutes after, Alix was called into his cabin. He was frantic, holding the piece of paper in his hand. "Look at that."

She took the note and read it:

I have information about the Ghost.
10pm, The Bell Inn. Come alone.

Though she did not have a personal grudge against the Ghost, she knew what he had done and embraced Vivien and the captain's need for justice. She felt a pang in her chest: this note could be the lead they had been waiting for for so long. She tampered her excitement. The 'come alone' was not a good sign.

"Isn't it great news? Finally, we will have some answers!" He looked so happy that she felt bad being the voice of reason.

"It might be a trap."

Surprised painted his face. "How so? What could they gain from that?"

She shrugged. "I don't know: maybe money, maybe to hurt you. My point is, you shouldn't go alone."

He shook his head. "I don't think so, and at this point, it doesn't matter either. I will go and I will find out information about the Ghost."

Seeing that he had his mind set and knowing how stubborn he could be, Alix caved in. "Fair enough, but don't go alone."

He shrugged and made a gesture of his hand to dismiss her concerns. "I'll be fine – I'm a pirate after all!" he added with a wink.

She stared coldly at him, her arms folded over her chest, but answered calmly. "Captain, this inn is on the outskirts of the town. Even if it isn't a trap, we both know that these streets aren't safe at night. Take a couple of people to accompany you on the road, please."

"Al, I know you are worried, but I'll be fine. I have been there before, I know the place and I know how to defend myself. If it's a trap, I'll not lead any member of my crew to be killed." She opened her mouth to object, but he added, his light blue eyes frostily staring at her, "This is an order."

Alix closed her mouth and pinched her lips. She was annoyed – no, furious. She turned on her heels and left the room without a word, not even turning back when he called her name.

Vivien did not come back with Evan – it was not uncommon; often crew members would spend an evening in the city's taverns or a night in a good bed – so Alix had to make a plan by herself. She did not care if the captain did not need help; she would make sure he stayed safe and sound. Resolved, she hid a couple of knives and a pistol in her clothing, draping herself in her dark cape then leaving for the inn before the captain. When he walked in, she was in the main room, her face concealed, a tankard of beer in front of her. That inn was such a hell hole that no one minded having people covering their face. The tables were full of drunk and smelly people, some drinking their sorrow alone, some in groups. A few prostitutes offered their services, sitting on potential clients' laps and laughing loudly at their drunken comments. Alix shrugged in disgust – it was not an environment she was comfortable being in, and she hoped that none of them would find out that she was a girl…

When he arrived, the captain sat at a table where a man had fallen asleep despite the noise and waited a bit for someone to come and talk to him. Gritting her teeth, Alix was waiting impatiently, one of her feet tapping, picking behind her hood to see if anyone made a move. Her short nails were playing on the metallic tankard, but the room was so loud that she could not even hear the sound. Finally, a tall man wearing a hood came to the captain, talking to him briefly before guiding him to the back. Something in that man, his way of walking, moving, seemed familiar. Maybe another pirate she had met before? Alix checked that no one was paying attention to her – the high level of alcohol in every person in the room helped – and followed them.

They went through a corridor and then a door. After waiting a bit, careful of not making any sound, Alix opened the door and ended up outside. A bit disoriented, she stayed immobile and looked around to find the men. A light flickering in the dark indicated that they were going away from the road in a secluded, if not deserted, area. *This isn't good*, she thought, worried, regretting not telling anyone else. *That was an ill-advised move. Stupid, stupid Alix! Why on earth did you have to be reckless?* Taking a knife in her hand, she started to walk in the direction taken by the men, careful not to make noise and to stay in the shadows as much as possible.

The walk was probably not long, but she was so focused on following them silently and carefully so as not to be noticed by anyone that it felt like it took hours. The warm air burned her skin and her heart was beating in her ears. She was half scared, half excited by the situation; in both cases, she knew it was a terrible idea, but at that point, she had no choice. Suddenly, she caught up to them and stopped dead in her tracks before hiding behind a tree. She was a bit far, but with the help of the torch, she could make out their facial features; or rather, she could see the captain fairly clearly, as the other man kept his hood up.

From then, they did not have to wait for a long time and some other men arrived. They were four, but only one of them came close enough – and without a hood – for Alix to see his face: middle-aged, round red face, dark hair. He nodded and asked straightforwardly, "Why are you interested in the *Ghost* and its captain?"

In the silence of this deserted area, the words came clearly to Alix. The man had an accent – French, she realised. *What a small world!*

The captain shrugged before answering. "I am just curious," he said cautiously.

The man had a dry smile and Alix knew he was not buying it, "Captain, we are between gentlemen – I do not appreciate you disrespecting me that way." Seeing the captain opening his mouth to refute this, he made a small, dismissive hand gesture. "Please, I know you've been looking for information, any information on the *Ghost* and its crew, for years." He stayed silent for a few seconds, letting it sink in. "If you want me to give you *any* information, you better be honest... So I'm gonna ask again: why are you interested in the *Ghost* and its captain?"

The captain stayed silent – Alix could almost see his brain weigh up the pros and cons. Would he say the full truth or just half of it? Would he lie? She was too far away to have a proper picture of the situation, but she could see the aggressive stance of the Frenchman and, though they were in the shadows, the others sent an aggressive vibe. She had a sinking feeling in her stomach and knew it was not going to end well. Even if she was not too far to help the captain if it became necessary, both of them would not cut it in front of five armed men.

She saw the attitude of the captain shift and he started to talk with numerous gestures of the arms to sell his story. "As you know, I'm the captain of a very profitable pirate ship myself and I've been wanting to meet the captain of the *Ghost* to talk about some business opportunities. We're doing good on our own, but imagine what we could do together..."

The captain was ready to carry on his pitch, but one of the men snorted and said something in French. The Frenchman turned towards him and nodded with deference, perhaps even a tinge of fear. *He is just a translator... so this crew is French. Could the Ghost be French too?*

The translator turned back and answered the captain. "This isn't the information we received."

Keeping his cool, the captain asked, "What information did you receive?"

"You've been looking for us for a long time and the key word we heard was 'revenge'."

Both Alix and the captain tensed up. 'Us' – so not only was this the crew of the Ghost but they were here to silence the captain. Alix was scared and angry: *I knew it was a trap!* Her shaking hand grabbed her pistol; she stood up and was ready to move when someone grabbed her, put a hand on her mouth and a knife on her throat.

"*Qu'avons-nous ici?*[11]" said a voice she thought she would never hear again. She froze.

The man removed her hood and turned her face towards him. She saw his eyes open widely in recognition; the knife became loose in his grip and he turned her to face him. None of them said anything, taking up the other one after so many years apart. She thought she had forgotten him, but now that they were face to face, her lingering feelings came back as a tidal wave. It was too dark to properly see his features, but she could see that his jaw had sharpened and his shoulders seemed larger – or was it that, after all this time, she had actually forgotten him? His empty hand came to cup her right cheek and she could not stop herself from leaning towards him. They got so close that she could feel his breath on her

11   What do we have here?

lips, but the moment exploded when they heard: "*Henri? Que se passe-t-il?*[12]"

Alix recognised the imperious voice of Jacques de Kerhoët and took a step back. Henri caught her hand and stopped her from walking out of the shadows.

"*Rien père, j'ai entendu un bruit, mais ce n'était qu'un chat.*[13]"

Alix could almost hear the Count – no, the Ghost – sigh in annoyance. "*Reviens alors!*[14]"

Henri turned but Alix grabbed his arm. "*Ne lui faites pas de mal.*[15]"

His caring expression turned blank; Alix realised that she did not know him at all. They had barely had a few encounters years ago and her feelings were based on the man she thought he was. It was apparently not the person he actually was.

"*Il est trop tard pour cela. Reste ici et ne fais pas de bruit, sinon il va te tuer aussi.*[16]"

She wanted to argue, to shout, to insult him, but she knew he was right and, more importantly, that the captain would not want for her to die here. Not now that she had all the keys to end the Ghost, to put an end to all their revenge. So she stayed hidden, watching Henri going back to his father and the other crew members. The argument did not last long: the Ghost clearly had set his mind on the outcome of the encounter way before he had met the captain. Smiling, he

12 What's happening?
13 Nothing, Father, I heard a noise but it was just a cat.
14 Come back then!
15 Do not hurt him.
16 It is too late for that. Stay here and stay quiet, otherwise he will kill you too.

stabbed the captain in his midsection, enough to kill but not enough to ensure a quick and painless death. His men stood there and watched whilst Alix bit her lips to swallow her shouts, tears streaming from her eyes. The Ghost and his men stayed a few minutes more, enjoying the captain's suffering, then left, one of them glancing longingly in Alix's direction – Henri, she assumed, but, at this point, she did not really care.

She waited to ensure that they would not come back; when she could not take it anymore, she ran to the captain. He was breathing painfully, his hands holding his belly, unable to stop the blood pouring. She put her hands on top of his and pressed down, which made him open his eyes.

"Alix! What the hell are you doing here?"

Frantic, she did not answer, looking around. "Can you walk? I'll help you get back to the ship and Pierre will fix you up."

"No need – I've lost too much blood and I won't make it."

"It's my fault – I should have come quicker, but I was afraid they were still around," answered a crying Alix, burying her face in the captain's shoulder.

"It's my fault and my fault only. You tried to warn me, but I didn't listen; I let my anger speak and now I'm dying without answers."

Alix sat back and dried her cheeks, blood mixing with her tears. "No, I know who he is. I know the Ghost's real identity."

The captain closed his eyes, his ragged breath becoming more erratic with the pain and the loss of blood. "You will avenge me then?" he asked in a strangely firm voice.

"Yes, I promise. Vivien and I will end him."

The captain slightly nodded and his face relaxed. "Good, there is now one more thing I need you to do for me…"

Vivien woke up with a heavy head. The light of the sun rising hurt her eyes and the rum she had drunk last night did not help. She felt a weight on her and realised she was sleeping in Evan's arms, probably in one of the rooms of the tavern they had gone in last night – again. She knew they should not do that, but every time they spent an evening together on land, they ended up having sex and then pretended nothing happened until the next time. It was already the fifth or sixth time and this was becoming a problem.

"Barely awake and already deep in thought," said Evan with a hoarse voice.

She turned towards him and saw that his eyes were not even open. "How did you know?"

"It's always the same… In a minute you'll say that we shouldn't do that and that it's the last time."

Vivien was stunned, both because he knew her that well and because of the bitter tone he used. She sat up on the bed and tried to rationalise the situation. "Well, we work on the same crew, so yes, we shouldn't do that."

Evan stayed silent. Vivien side-glanced at him: he was lying on his back, one hand behind his head, the other on his chest. His electric blue eyes were staring at her. She shivered, painfully aware of her nakedness. Annoyance left his eyes to be replaced with desire as they hungrily roamed her body. His signature cocky smile appeared on his lips. "In that case, we should say goodbye."

He immediately pulled Vivien on top of him, his mouth

on hers, his hands exploring her naked back. As the kiss deepened, she started to think that she could get used to saying goodbye.

Later that morning, they both came back on the *Mermaid*. They were not the only ones who had spent the night onshore, so their arrival did not trigger any comments – to Vivien's relief. She went straight to the sleeping quarters she shared with Alix, but there was no one there. She went to the captain's cabin, but it was also empty. She went around the ship looking for any of them, asking the sailors she saw questions: no one had seen the captain and Alix since the prior evening and she was starting to worry. She knew they were grown up, trained and probably armed, but something was off; they would have never gone anywhere without letting the crew know. Vivien could not shake off the insidious feeling that made her stomach heave.

Daniela came back, reeking of alcohol, her eyes bloodshot. "Have you seen the captain or Alix?"

The girl grunted – ever since the first day, she'd disliked Vivien, for reasons known only to herself. She tried to move away, but Vivien grabbed her arm and asked in a menacing voice, "No one has seen them since yesterday and I am slowly getting pissed off that no one knows anything. So I am asking again: have you seen the captain or Alix?"

Daniela shrugged. "They didn't tell me anything obviously, but the captain got a message and Alix was the one who took it to him."

Vivien frowned. "When was that?"

"Yesterday afternoon, after you left with Evan." Vivien

ignored the other girl's smirk and the tone she used – she would deal later with the gossip. Daniela added, snarky, "Can I go now?"

Vivien let go of her arm – she had not realised that she was still holding it – and rushed to the captain's cabin, followed by Daniela's swearing. On the desk, there was a half-full bottle of rum, an empty glass and a crumbled piece of paper. Even if Vivien had been jealous of Alix's literacy, she had never really felt the need to learn how to read and she regretted it now. She dashed out, going to Pierre – the only one on board who could read.

Breathless, she barged in his room and gave him the paper. "What does it say?"

"*I have information about the Ghost. 10pm, The Bell Inn. Come alone.*" As she swore, he looked puzzled. "What's that?"

"The captain and Alix are missing, and I found that note in his cabin…"

"Do you think they went there alone?" asked Pierre, alarmed.

Vivien nodded. "Unfortunately, yes – it's been so long… You know that he would have done anything to have a shred of information about the Ghost."

"Aye, even if it cost him his life."

Pierre's comment echoed Vivien's worst fear.

"Let's go."

On their way out of the ship, they saw Evan, and Vivien asked him to come with them.

"Why would they go there? The Bell Inn is a cutthroat place – no one goes there without anything to hide."

Pierre nodded. "Aye, it's not good…"

They walked as fast as they could and, when they arrived at the inn, they searched every single room – without luck. They woke up every drunkard to ask them questions, but none of them had a clear recollection of the night before. Vivien's worrying had been steadily growing since they had left the ship and it was now peaking; Evan placed his hand on her back and the soothing gesture relieved her a bit.

"We should look around," suggested Pierre.

The two others agreed and they started exploring the paths around the inn. They had been at it for some time when Evan, who was walking ahead, stopped in his tracks. He turned to signal for them to come closer and Vivien saw that his face had gone white. She started to run and saw, in the middle of a small clearing, Alix sitting motionless, holding the hand of the captain. Even from afar, she could see the knife coming out of his chest. She felt sick but did not stop until she arrived at the scene. Except for the blade and the blood, the captain had his eyes closed and looked peaceful; Alix was staring ahead, her eyes swollen but dry. Keeping her sadness at bay, Vivien kneeled in front of her, putting her hands on Alix's shoulders.

"Al, are you alright? What happened?"

Evan was looking around for some clues while Alix remained motionless and speechless. Vivien shot a concerned glance at Pierre, he came closer and attempted to get Alix's attention. "Al, can you hear me?"

Once more, she did not flinch or make a noise. Her eyes were empty and her body frozen; even her skin was cold. Pierre looked at her but only saw blood on her hands and face.

"Is she hurt?" asked Vivien.

Pierre shook his head. "Nay, the blood seems to be his. I don't know what happened here, but she saw it and she's in shock. I've only seen someone reacting like that once and there isn't much we can do, except be there for her and ensure her safety."

"I see." Vivien then turned to Evan. "Go back to the inn and see if there is a cart and a horse we can use to bring them back to the ship. Of course we will pay for it."

Evan nodded and darted towards the inn. He came back several minutes after with a man who was clearly annoyed to be awaken again from his drunken slumber. Before he could even start to complain, Vivien came towards him. "You'll help us and not say a word – in exchange, as soon as we are back at our ship, we'll give you a gold piece." The man opened his eyes wide and nodded. "Good, let's put them in the cart and go."

That same evening, the ship sailed towards Hope. Normally, a captain would rest in the ocean, but it felt right for him to rest on land, in the town he had helped create, surrounded by people who cared about him. During the journey, Alix stayed in the captain's cabin, lying on his bed, barely eating and drinking, and not saying a word. She was not even crying. Vivien was angry both at the murderers and at Alix for being so helpless; she had to step up and take control, keeping her own grief at bay. Some nights, she would go to the figurehead and Evan would come offering her his shoulder to cry on. He knew she needed it but could not show any weakness to the rest of the crew. By the time they arrived, Joseph, the

Mermaid's carpenter, had had the time to build a coffin for the captain – it was far from his usual job, but he insisted on doing it for the man he had admired most.

The news was a shock for everyone; Charlotte shouted and insulted Alix, who did not react. Only when Peter came with his joyous babble, unaware of what happened, did she start to move. Seeing the little boy, her son, was a shock for her and she slowly came back to life. Yet no one pressed her for answers; the most important thing was to say a proper goodbye to the captain.

On the day of his funeral, the little place was full of people wanting to pay their respects. Holding Peter by one hand, Alix came to stand near Vivien and reached out to take her hand; the latter wanted to resist, but the pleading look in her friend's eyes dissuaded her from doing so. It was not the time to hold grudges. The ceremony was followed by a dinner and an evening of drinks in the honour of the captain.

The following day, Alix asked the crew and the captain's family to meet with her. Finally back to her normal self, she kept on fidgeting until everyone was there. Anxious, she cleared her throat and asserted, "The captain was killed by the Ghost."

Everyone gasped and Charlotte answered, annoyed, "Don't be ridiculous! Why would the Ghost come from God knows where to kill my husband?"

"Because he's a sick bastard!" snapped Alix before explaining what had happened, from the time she had received the letter to the moment she had stabbed the captain in the heart – with his blessing – to stop his suffering. "I promised to avenge him…" She stopped talking, her voice breaking. Pierre and Vivien put their hands on each of her arms.

Hardly believing that story, Charlotte added, "You're back to square one, dear – no lead and no captain."

Alix dried her tears with the back of her hand. "For the captain, I vote that we elect Vivien as our captain. Who's in favour?"

A concert of 'aye's exploded in the room.

"Against?"

A few 'nay's were heard, but clearly not enough.

Alix nodded. "Good, our crew has a new captain. Then I should add that our captain didn't die in vain: I saw the Ghost and I know who he is and where he lives. So if you're all up for it, I have a plan to have our revenge."

The room looked at her, stunned, before erupting in cheers. Alix had a sad smile; the next months were going to be challenging to say the least. She squared her shoulders and knew it would be worth it.

NINE

January 1696

Alix was in front of the castle's door. A part of her had hoped she would never be here again, but she had made a promise and she was not going to bail out. Her thoughts wandered towards Thérèse and the captain, both dead because of the selfishness of the Kerhoëts. If it was even possible, her resolve to make them pay for their deceit, their cruelty and the death of her loved ones grew even more. She straightened her back, squared her shoulders – *The show is about to start* – and walked through the entrance of Beg Hastel. It was cold and rainy, and she was happy to be wearing the nun's robe – unfashionable but thick enough to not let the rain go through. She rang the bell and waited for the door to open. The maid was vaguely familiar – Françoise, Fanchette or Francine – and, most importantly, recognised her immediately. She remained motionless, her mouth open and her eyes wide.

Alix took a deep breath, looked down and plastered a sweet smile on her face. "Can I see the Countess de Kerhoët, please?" she asked timidly.

The maid nodded and made her stay in the entrance. She came back a few minutes after. "Please follow me."

Alix remembered the first time she had come in this house, how scared and impressionable she had been... Now she could see it for what it was: an old and dark castle, full of secrets and deceit – and she was more than ready to play her part and destroy this house of cards. Alix entered one of the sitting rooms, keeping her eyes on the floor. She knew the Countess was there, so she bowed and did not get up, to make her believe that she was meek and repentant.

"Seeing you here is truly a surprise..." started the Countess with a cold voice. Alix bowed deeper but did not answer. "Care to tell me where you've been?"

The young woman briefly closed her eyes and took a big breath in. "I... I was scared by the perspective of marriage. I went to find shelter in the abbacy of Port-Royal-des-Champs where my sister Agnès was already a nun. As you know, my faith is very strong and I felt I should dedicate my life to please the Lord rather than a husband."

The Countess laughed joylessly. "Then what are you doing here?"

Alix did not fail to notice that the Countess had not asked her to stand up. She was testing her and, even though her muscles started to warm up and soon would become painful, the young woman did not move as she answered, "After extensive prayers, I realised that I'd made a mistake. God wanted me to marry your son and it was wrong of me to reject His plan." Alix decided to provide a more selfish reason. She paused and added, "I also discovered that life in a nunnery isn't for me, and I hope you'll find it in your heart to forgive my reckless behaviour."

She could feel more than see the Countess smiling and sensed some sort of satisfaction radiating from her. She probed a bit further. "Why not go to your father?"

Alix started wringing her hand, feigning despair. "I dishonoured him and the Lecuyer name when I left. I can only assume that you told him about my shameful behaviour and I cannot bear to see or contact him before righting my wrongs towards you and your family."

The Countess snorted. "So coming back and marrying my son is just about 'righting your wrongs'?"

Alix closed her eyes: *Time to perform!* She took a deep breath, thinking of the captain to make her tears flow. She then looked up, her face wet and anguished. She knew she must be quite a sight with her tearful eyes, her pleading face, her modest dress sprawled around her like a gloomy flower; she spoke with a cracking voice. "I was young and stupid; I didn't understand that what I felt was love. I... I think I was scared by the intensity of what I felt for Louis and your family; I was unable to understand my feelings and I ran away – a sin I shall forever be atoning for. I am here now to plead for your forgiveness, make amends and join your family, if you'll still have me."

The shock followed by thoughtfulness that painted the Countess's face told Alix that she had been convincing. Louise nodded. "Stand up, Fanchette will bring you to your room. We need to wait for the Count before making any decision regarding the wedding. Dinner is at seven as usual."

Knowing she was dismissed, Alix stood up – hiding the sharp pain she felt when she moved – bowed down and went back her old room. She had expected the chests to be empty, but she was wrong and her old clothes were still there. She smiled: the long game had started…

The *Mermaid* was berthed in the harbour of Lorient with a skeleton crew. Vivien did not like to leave her for too long, but for the – *stupid and dangerous* – plan they had all agreed on, they must be near Beg Hastel. Alix was right about one thing: the view from the Breton coast was breath-taking. Evan and Vivien posed as a wealthy English couple, Pierre as their translator and the rest of the crew their servants. They had rented a small manor near Beg Hastel and were ready to move to the second phase of the plan, when they would get the signal: the announcement of the wedding. The pirates had arrived near Beg Hastel about a week before Alix had reappeared at the castle and they had used the time to spy on the property and its people, identify weaknesses and the best roads to take to flee, day and night.

Too much of the plan was resting on Alix's shoulders and Vivien did not like that. Not that she doubted her friend's abilities, but she was afraid it was too much for her or that something would go wrong… Since they parted, the *Mermaid*'s captain had been restless and anxious. So much was at stake. So much could go wrong. And every time her feelings overpowered her spirits, she reasoned with herself: even if they failed, Alix had prepared many letters to send to their friends and families so the world would know who the Ghost was and he would get what he deserved one way or another. This thought never failed to calm her. Now, Vivien was becoming impatient to say the least. Eight long years she had been waiting to avenge Michael; she had sacrificed her family and her chance to have a normal life; her adoptive father had been murdered. She had lost so much and, now that it was happening, she could not help wonder if it had been worth it. *It was*, she thought. *It must be.*

"Stop overthinking!" ordered Evan from the door.

She turned and he joined her by the fire. She shook her head to cast aside her doubts and questions. "You never said what your beef with the Ghost was," she prompted him, to take her mind off the situation.

Evan sat on the couch, his long legs stretched towards the fire. "I didn't have any until he killed the captain."

She looked at him, surprised. "Why did you join his crew then?"

He shrugged. "I'm a thief, Vi. My destiny was to die at the end of a rope. The captain saw me and, for some reason, offered me a place in his crew. I don't know why, he didn't tell me, but I owe him my life."

She could see what the captain had seen in him: his resourcefulness, even temper, good humour and, despite his habit of stealing, his goodness. She answered, "Well, you can still end up being hanged for being a pirate..."

He flashed her his bright smile, his eyes sparkling – or maybe it was just the reflection of the fire. In any case, the effect was startling and Vivien's heart started to beat a bit faster.

"True, but that led me to you, so I'm fine with it."

Vivien blushed and stared at him awkwardly. It sounded like a love declaration, didn't it? Was she reading too much into it? Was he expecting an answer? What was she supposed to do? She wished Alix was around to talk about it. Not that her friend was helpful – she was even more clueless than her – but at least Vivien would be able to voice her questions.

As if reading her mind, Evan softly laughed and put his arm around her shoulder, bringing her closer to him. "As I said, don't overthink it!"

She tensed before relaxing. She decided that it did not have to mean anything and they had a lot of time to kill, so she turned his head towards hers and started to kiss him. That way no unwanted thought would come to pollute her mind.

The Count and Henri came back ten days after Alix. During that time, she kept up the act of the fiancée in love, the repentant daughter-in-law, the long-lost friend and the pious girl – even though all of them disgusted her. Despite believing in God, she had not prayed as much as she used to and her faith had evolved; she did not fully believe in Jansenism as she had before. Yet, the old habits came back easily to her and she spent several hours a day praying. Louis did not care much of her return – on the contrary, it appeared that she had spoiled his fun and he seemed to resent her. *A bad omen for our upcoming nuptials*, she thought with a smile. His barely hidden hostility only made her feel more resentful toward him. Playing the enamoured fiancée and seeing him scolded by his mother every time he showed his attitude of disinterest – if not repulsion – was very entertaining for Alix. The hateful glances he shot her fully displayed that he intended to make her pay when they got married, and she hoped the plan would go smoothly. Fake Marguerite seemed happy, but Alix did not trust her enough to let her guard down; she was not a naïve girl anymore and was not going to let that liar manipulate her. The only one who was genuinely happy to see her was Marguerite – she had bought books in Lorient for her – and she went to see her several times those first days.

Her heart was beating fast on her way to dinner; she knew the Ghost would be there and she had to convince him. She assumed that the Countess had already reported everything about her return, but whatever they thought her motivations were in coming back, they could not guess the truth – *except if Henri babbled*. That was the weakness of her plan, the one thing she had not told the others. And she knew why. Verbalising what had happened between them would force her to put a name to feelings she had hoped to forget. Even before she realised he was the Ghost's son, they could not have a future together. Believing so was just another sign of her naivety and foolishness. But now, after everything that had happened, and after everything that would happen, any relationship between them would be impossible.

She sighed and entered the room, the conversation dying instantly; she was surrounded by a heavy silence as she went to her place. She avoided everyone's eyes but mostly Henri's. Yet she could not stop herself from noticing that he was glaring at her, his jaws clenched. She bowed down and sat, crossing her hands on her lap and looking down, attempting to be as inconspicuous as possible. Soon the talk rekindled, but, she suspected, with a different topic. As usual with this family, dinner was long and boring, filled with too many dishes that the young woman could barely touch.

Only at the dessert did the Count address her with his cold voice. "Back with us, I can see – you've finished with your shenanigans, silly girl?"

A cold chill ran down her spine and she forced herself to stay immobile. "Indeed, sir, I've realised my foolishness and I'm humbly asking to be a part of your family, if you'd have me." The room was silent for a few minutes and she could feel everyone's eyes on her, which rattled Alix's nerves.

"Look at me," said the Count.

Praying that she was being convincing, she raised her eyes, trying to look as innocent, lost and anxious as possible – the last bit was the easiest one. It worked and the Count had a cold smile. "I forgive you; we forgive you. The wedding will be next Sunday."

She gasped. "It's less than a week to prepare…"

His smile vanished and he fixed her with a hard stare. "My son has been waiting long enough, hasn't he?"

She blushed and lowered her head, as if defeated. "Indeed, sir, I wouldn't want to make him wait… My surprise was just regarding the publication of the wedding notice in the papers…"

"Don't worry about that – I'll speak with the priest and it won't be an issue," retorted the Count.

Alix hesitated, unsure that it was the right moment, but she had to try. "May I ask for a favour?"

"What is it?" he snapped back, and her immediate reaction was to recoil, which made her furious and ashamed. Yet it served her purpose, as the Count could not stop a smile from blooming on his lips.

"As my family will not be here, could we invite some of

the neighbours…?" She trailed off and shook her head, her palms sweaty. "Don't mind me, it was a silly idea."

"No, it isn't!" interjected fake Marguerite, always happy to be around people. "Father, please say yes. It would be good to socialise with our peers; also, I've heard there are a couple of wealthy English people who've moved in not far away – it would be nice to make their acquaintance. It has been so long since we had a party!"

Whilst the Count and the Countess exchanged a glance, Alix held her breath; so much of the plan depended on that. When he reluctantly nodded, she relaxed – not too noticeably so as to not raise their distrust. Yet, one quick glance at Henri told her that, for him, she was more than suspicious.

"This seem like a good idea; everyone will be able to rejoice with us on that happy day. Marguerite, you'll be in charge of organising the reception," concluded the Countess with a sly smile when her fake daughter's face fell.

Alix bit the inside of her cheeks to hide her smile. Everything was falling into its place and the fact that fake Marguerite was given some extra work was an added bonus for her.

Alix waited for everyone to go to sleep and slipped out her room to go see Marguerite. Her light was on – the poor girl did not sleep much and was bored in her tower. Used to the trip to the North Tower by now, the young woman did not need a candle; she just had to be careful that no one else was up and around – which was almost never the case. At night, Beg Hastel was as dark and silent as a sepulchre; it had scared her at first but now she had learnt to appreciate it. And it made any unwelcome presence easy to discern and avoid. A couple of times she had almost run into Louis coming from the servant quarters, leaving in his trail a smell of alcohol and some poor whistling. Those nights, it took everything she had in her to stay hidden and not stab him to death as he deserved. She felt anger and hate surge into her just at the thought of it. She closed her eyes and took a deep breath to clear her head before entering Marguerite's room; the poor girl did not need any more negativity in her life.

"Good evening! What are you reading?" said Alix as she entered the room.

Marguerite was sitting in a comfortable armchair, her feet on a stool. She was so engrossed in her book that she did not realise that her friend had come in. She showed her the first page of the book: *Britannicus* by Jean Racine.

"This is joyous, dear…" commented Alix.

Marguerite shrugged. "Would you prefer the *Princesse de Clèves*?"

Alix rolled her eyes. "Don't you have anything less gloomy? Some plays by Molière for instance?"

Marguerite shrugged. "My life isn't a comedy – why should I try to make it better?"

Alix frowned, unhappy that their conversation had become so dark. She realised that Marguerite was wildly hopeless about her situation – everyone would be – and she did not know how to help her. She tried: "Because without hope, there is no life…"

Marguerite let out a joyless laugh. "What life? I have been locked in a tower for so many years that I don't even remember what it feels like to walk on the grass or feel sand between my toes."

Alix hesitated for a second; she had never seen her friend so low. She had to give her a shred of hope, so she took a deep breath and prayed that she would make the right decision. She came closer and took one of Marguerite's hands. "If I offered you a way out, would you take it? I know a place where you could be free to be who you want to be."

Marguerite looked both intrigued and doubtful; she asserted, "There is no way out."

"There is." After a short silence, Alix added with an intense look, "If you are ready to pay the price."

Startled, Marguerite frowned. "What price? My family would never allow me to leave…" She saw something on Alix's face and realisation washed over her. "Oh, that kind of price."

She stayed silent for a long time, weighing up her options. "I wish I could be in a position to say that I never want any harm come upon my family, but none of them – with the exception of Henri – cared for me, quite the opposite…" The words died in her mouth, but she quickly shook her head and put a determined look on her face. "I will leave this place, whatever the cost."

Alix nodded and squeezed her hand. "Have a bag prepared on Sunday."

Marguerite opened her eyes widely. "On your wedding day?"

"Yes, I don't want anything to do with your family and on Sunday I'll be leaving."

"Except me," asked Marguerite with a tentative smile.

Alix hugged her. "Of course except you, you're the best of them!"

They talked more after that, Marguerite fired up by her prospective freedom. She was bubblier than Alix had ever seen her, which convinced her that she had made the right decision in including her in the plan. She left her friend and was going back to her room when someone grabbed her , put a hand on her mouth and brought her to a dusky and dusty room barely lit by the moonlight coming through a small window. She was afraid to have been caught and her heart was beating fast, but, mixed with the dirt, she smelled a familiar scent and relaxed.

"It feels like a déjà vu," said Henri in a low voice with a hint of a smile.

She opened her mouth and bit his palm which led to him releasing her and swearing.

"That wasn't necessary!"

She crossed her arms on her chest and replied, "But you grabbing me was?"

It was too dark to see his features properly, just like the previous time, and she could not look at him with his family around, fearing that she would drop the act. He swore a bit more before calming down. He came closer, backing her up against the wall and, even though she could not see them properly, she felt his eyes watching her intensely, almost burning her skin.

"Why are you here?"

"Visiting a friend."

"Alix," he grunted in a low voice, "you were a silly girl and I fear you've become a silly woman."

"If only I cared about your opinion," she snapped back.

Even though she could not see him, surprised painted on

his face, soon replaced with a delighted smile. This woman was more than just silly, and he enjoyed his banter with her.

"Which friend are you visiting?"

She sighed and answered, "Rapunzel – she let down her hair to allow me into her tower."

Henri froze and stayed silent for some time, Alix smiling smugly at him. Squinting his eyes, he put his hands on each side of her face. She knew it was meant to be threatening, but, despite everything that had happened, she was certain that he would never hurt her, so she carried on smiling.

"How did you find out?" he asked curtly.

She shrugged. "Contrary to what you and your family think, I am not stupid." He opened his mouth to contradict her, but she kept on speaking, perhaps not even noticing his attempt. "You were there when I saw the light at the top of the tower. Did you really think I would not investigate? Especially after seeing that light more than once?" She crossed her arms over her chest. "If so, you are truly delusional.

He mumbled something about him not being the most delusional one in the room. Then, he came closer, pressing their bodies against each other, and asked again, "Why are you here?"

"It doesn't matter, and get away from me," and yet she did not move or try to make him move.

Despite the obscurity, she saw him smirk. "Am I bothering you?"

"No, I just don't want to be close to you."

"And why is it that?" he asked, still smiling and caressing her cheek.

"Because I've seen the man you are and I would rather not

be close to you," she answered, looking straight in his eyes.

His smiled disappeared, his body tensed and he took a step back. She immediately felt cold and lonely. He stayed silent for a bit before adding, "What you think of me doesn't matter; you shouldn't be here."

She slid away and started to walk back to her room. He followed her and grabbed her arm. "Alix, you must leave. Nothing has changed; their plan is the same as it was five years ago."

"I know," she turned to face him, "but this time I have a plan too, and nothing, or no one, will stop me."

"What will you do?" he asked in a low voice.

She shook her head. "Do you actually believe that I would tell you anything?" She laughed. "You truly are delusional!"

He grunted and whispered, angry, "I am on your side!"

She came closer and tapped on his chest with her finger. "You are on your father's side and no one else's—"

"I helped you leave," he answered in a voice in which anger and hurt were mixed.

"You made a kind gesture once, but it didn't cost you anything. You have been watching your father murdering hundreds of innocent men for no reason… As they say, the road to hell is paved with good intentions."

He stepped back, as if she had punched him. "This isn't fair – I didn't have a choice or a say in this," he answered weakly.

"We always have a choice; you are not a child, Henri! You chose not to stop your father from murdering one of the most honourable men I have ever met. You chose to let that man slowly bleed out to death." She was just whispering, but in the complete silence of the tower, it sounded like shouting. She felt the tears building in the corner of her eyes, but she was unable to stop the words. "I chose to end his suffering, regardless of the pain I have to live with for the rest of my life."

It was too much for Alix: her voice cracked and she started to cry – her anger vanished in the guilt and hurt she felt. Henri took her in his arms and caressed her hair to soothe her; and it worked. A part of her despised herself for betraying her family and her belief by being so weak around him, for feeling safe and almost at peace in his arms.

"I am so sorry, nothing I'll ever do can pay for the evil my family has done, but I promise that I'll help you, no matter the cost."

Once more, Alix took a step back, her hands straight on his chest, and looked up to see his face. She could feel his heart beating fast under her right palm. "Don't make that promise, you'll regret it."

He leaned forward and their foreheads touched, his hands surrounding her waist. "Whatever it is, I don't think I will."

They stayed together in silence for some time, basking in each other's warmth and comfort, until Alix took a step back. Henri did not let her go yet but did not say anything. Her heart was beating fast; she had a choice to make and was not sure if it was the right one. Henri was immobile, just observing her and waiting for her decision, whatever it was. He had long ago decided that he would do anything for her, and he would keep his word regardless of where it led him. Alix tilted her head back and kissed him. Henri's surprise was short and he answered the kiss quickly, sliding one hand round the back of her neck and pressing their bodies together as close as he could. They kissed as if it was the last time, pouring all of their feelings into it. When they parted, breathless, Alix managed to say, "Let's go to my room," before she walked away, holding firmly his hand in hers.

If Henri was surprised, he did not show anything. He did not object either, more than willingly following her.

A couple of hours later, they rested in each other's arms, limbs tangled, their hearts beating at the same pace. Her head on the crook of his right arm, Alix finally broke the comfortable silence.

"If everything goes as I planned," she did not trust him enough to mention her crew, even though he probably knew they would be involved, "I'll take Marguerite with me."

He tensed for a second before relaxing. "You are right: she deserves a good and happy life." He raised his head to look at Alix. "Can you promise me you will take care of her?"

She shifted her position, her chest on top of his and their eyes on the same level. "I promise. I know a place where she will be free to be whoever she wants to be without judgement."

Henri nodded, tears forming in his eyes. "Thank you."

Alix bit her lower lip, hesitating. She wanted to tell him about Peter, to tell him he had a nephew and that Marguerite would never be lonely in Hope with them. But their relationship – if it could ever be considered as such – was not only a sin but also doomed from the start. Regardless of how the plan went on Sunday, there would be no future for them, no possibility to meet again, no happy ending. Their love – even though none of them had said anything, Alix knew that it could only be love – was not meant to be, and as much as it broke her heart, it also made every second they could spend together a thousand times more real and intense than everything she had ever felt.

"Is anything wrong?" asked Henri, concerned by the serious look on her face.

Pushing back her feelings and sad prospects of a future without him, Alix put a cheeky smile on her face and said, "Yes, I was thinking that we really aren't making the most of the time we have."

He smiled back and his hands roamed her back from her shoulders to her bottom. "Then we shall be more proactive."

She could not answer that, too busy responding to his urgent kiss.

The following day, a few miles from Beg Hastel, Vivien was waiting for something to happen in the living room of the rented manor. Anything. She did not mind: a fire, an earthquake or a flooding. Anything else other than this excruciating wait, doubled with the gloom of a raining January with its grey sky and sudden gush of winds. Staying idle in the house was tormenting for her and she even wished that she had learnt to read, so she would have something to pass the time. Evan's absence – he went to hunt and refused to let her come with him, arguing that it was unbecoming for a lady to spend her day in a forest, dressed like a game warden; he was aware he would sleep in his own room that night – made the time go even slower. Though, thinking of all the torture she could inflict on him was a truly enjoyable pastime. A noise at the door made her snap her head to look, desperately hoping for some news or entertainment.

"Did you hear, Milady? There will be a wedding at Beg Hastel next Sunday," said a smiling Pierre. Since they had moved here, they decided to always behave according to their character, even in private, in order not to make a stupid mistake when they were with other people. He showed Vivien a letter before quickly opening it and reading it out loud.

"How delightful, they've invited us to the wedding," she said with a wicked smile.

"Splendid, I will have all the necessities prepared for the big day," answered Pierre.

Sighing with relief and anticipation, Vivien sat back on the couch, her mind now fully dedicated to reviewing the plan and everything that could go wrong.

TEN

Sunday 29th January 1696

It was not dawn yet when Alix woke up, Henri's warm body cuddling her back, his arm holding her; his steady breathing was the only noise in the silent room. It took only a few days for her to get used to him sleeping on her side, holding her. It had been just a few days and she knew it would be very hard for her to go back to her normal life. She knew he should leave soon, but she did not want to move or wake him up. She wanted to be filled with this happiness a bit longer, as, when his arm was around her, she forgot the plan, the risks and the loneliness that would follow. And she wanted nothing more than to stay like that forever, basking in his warmth, smelling his unique scent and being soothed by his steady breath. Soft lips pressed on her neck brought her back to the present.

"Stop overthinking," said Henri, his voice laced with sleep, which did not stop him from holding tighter on to her and bringing her body closer to his.

"I don't," she lied.

She could feel him smile against the skin of her neck. "You're a terrible liar!"

It crossed her mind that if she was such a bad liar, his dad would have killed her already, but she did not say it. She could not bear to ruin the moment. So she rolled to face him, put her hand on his cheek and smiled. "Only you can see through my lies."

He rolled his eyes as she laughed, before kissing her palm. "Please, anyone could see through *that* lie."

She put her leg on his hip. "I'm so sorry, sir, did I offend you?" she asked, flapping her lashes, her arm around his waist.

He grunted before smiling, his blue eyes sparkling. "Very much so." He rolled on top of her. "What do you have in mind to wash away that wrongdoing?

She stayed silent for a few seconds, pretending to think, her fingertips grazing his back. "I think I will have to settle to whatever you think will be appropriate to right my wrong."

He suddenly looked serious. "Your whole life would not be enough." Her heart skipped a beat. "But I guess I will have to settle for whatever time we have left."

Unable to speak, she nodded and he started to kiss her. Even if they did not speak of it, they both knew it would be the very last time, and she barely managed to stop her tears from falling and ruining the moment.

A few hours later Alix, the Countess and fake Marguerite were getting ready, and the least that could be said was that the young woman's wedding dress was not great. She looked at herself in the mirror and tried not to look too disappointed – after all, it was not going to be her real wedding, but it truly was an ugly dress. The garment was a hand-me-down from the Countess, a green dress about twenty years out of fashion, hastily – and poorly – altered to Alix's measurements. The skirt was too long, the bodice not fitted enough and nothing had been done for the old-fashioned sleeves. As fake Marguerite and the Countess were in the room with her, she plastered a large smile on her face and did her best to pretend she was happy.

The Countess was observing her every move, so she could not show her real feelings regarding the despicable garment; she would have been too happy. Alix was quite certain that her future mother-in-law chose that dress on purpose, so she just had to pretend that she liked it. The quick but noticeable sight of disappointment on the Countess's face was a good enough reward. However, Alix found that playing the meek girl was easy compared to the happy bride, especially when the tension was slowly building: today was the end when all loose ends would be tied, or when hell would break loose. At least the wedding was a good enough cover for being nervous.

"You look so anxious, Alix!" Fake Marguerite giggled, echoing the young woman's thoughts.

Alix forced a smile and said in a slow voice, "It isn't every day that you get married…"

Fake Marguerite smiled more broadly and added with a wink, "I bet you are anxious for the wedding night."

Alix knew that would not happen, and it was not that prospect but her stolen moments with Henri that made her blush. She felt ridiculous, but it served her role.

"Marguerite, don't be so lewd," scolded the Countess. Hearing that, Alix almost smiled; the woman was probably not the only promiscuous woman in the room. Even though she should have been used to being put down by her father's wife, fake Marguerite did not answer. She was aware that she had neither the brain nor the wit to win against the Countess, so the girl sat on the bed and decided to sulk. Louise turned her attention to Alix, arranging the old lace and pearl veil – the Countess had worn it on her wedding day; she was adamant that it was a family heirloom that needed to be treated with the utmost delicacy – on her head and putting a small bouquet of pansies and violas in her hands. "You look as presentable as possible, all things considered. Let's go to the castle's chapel for the wedding."

Alix nodded and followed both women down the corridors, her heart beating fast and her hands sweaty.

The chapel was small and cold. Vivien examined the ancient place: the dark walls were damp, the windows were small and the scant candles did not bring nearly enough light. Alix had mentioned that, despite the murders and the looting, they were poor, so maybe they could not afford too many candles. Or maybe it was on purpose, to hide the disarrayed state of the chapel. Though it was small, the guests were scattered around the room. They seemed to know each other, but, for a reason unknown to Vivien, they did not mingle with each other. A nearby guest loudly sneezed, which got him a sharp look from Count de Kerhoët, the infamous Ghost. Alix had told her what he looked like, but she could not stop herself from finding him quite banal with his blond hair and blue eyes, and his average height and weight. Maybe Vivien had seen him in a street or a harbour and had not noticed him. It was only when their eyes crossed that she understood: they were as cold as the chapel, unforgiving and calculating. She realised now why the guests barely spoke: they probably did not want to cross the Count. Vivien's breath was stuck in her chest until he averted his gaze.

She had expected armed men to defend the Ghost, but there were just a few servants – some muscular, but most not. He seemed to be so convinced that no one would ever attack him that he had no one to protect him. She wondered, where was his crew? Would he be that overconfident – or careless – to allow his men to leave the ship and their captain when they were on land? And where was the ship? Alix had mentioned coves and caves in the cliffs; perhaps it was hidden there. Or, like the pirates, they had managed to disguise enough the ship to stay undetected in a harbour. Vivien felt a chill on her back at the thought that the Ghost's ship could be in Lorient, near the *Mermaid*. She shook her head to disperse the disturbing thoughts and resumed her survey of the room, its exits and its security. Maybe without the presence of unsuspecting guests, the Ghost would have had guards, but there were just some random strangers in their home – no doubt here for the entertainment and the stories they would tell their friends. She surveyed the room; there were about twenty guests. She smiled, already relishing the instant when she would fire on him and see his blood flow.

"Don't smile like that, you are creepy," whispered Evan.

She rolled her eyes and elbowed him. He smiled and took her hand. A lady sitting on the same row saw the gesture and made a comment that Vivien could not understand, but she saw Pierre – who was standing on the side – smile. She knew it was not bad or mean, but she could not wait to be back in a country where everyone spoke the same language as her and where she could understand the random comments made about her.

They did not have to wait long before seeing Alix come to the altar, near a handsome, but somewhat sleazy, young man. She glanced anxiously at her friends, who smiled encouragingly – everything and everyone was in place. Neither Vivien nor Evan could understand French, so the ceremony was extremely long and boring. They stood when everyone stood and even pretended to sing melodies they'd never heard before. When it was finally over, Vivien did not miss the tension and the brief disgusted expression on Alix's face when her new husband kissed her. She also saw myriad feelings quickly passing over the other son of the Ghost's face: anger, hate, sadness and resignation. Vivien also noticed that when the newlyweds left the chapel, the new bride exchanged a look with her brother-in-law. She sighed, hoping that it would not put the plan in jeopardy. She reminded herself that Alix had proven her dedication to the *Mermaid*, the memory of the captain and the plan. She trusted her and knew she would not do anything to endanger any of her crewmates.

A small party on the honour of the newlyweds was organised in one of the receptions of the castle, and Vivien was trying hard not to look impressed, but it was by far the biggest and oldest fortress she had ever seen. It was dark, not very clean and sparsely decorated, and yet it exuded strength, pride and history. Vivien knew that if the walls could talk they would have thousands of interesting stories to narrate. Knowing where she was coming from made her feel small and insignificant amongst the stones and the story. She also realised that it was being born and raised in such a place that made the Ghost and his family feel above everyone else and made them believe they could do anything they wanted without consequences. The richer they were, the less empathy they had for everyone. For a second, she remembered the slave ship on which she used to work, where sailors with a poor background still considered the black people they transported as their inferior – worse, as mere merchandise, less than nothing. She thought that, in the end, humans always had to find someone to consider lesser then them. But today, she was going to be the one making history, showing these noble people and their bloody castle that their inferiors should not be underappreciated.

Evan nudged her out of her daydreaming. "Would you like a glass of cider, dear?"

He spoke with his formal tone and vocabulary, the same ones they had used to joke in the manor, so Vivien was startled for a second before answering, "Yes, my darling, but do not worry, I will fetch one myself; I need to stretch my legs." She wondered why that masquerade was necessary, as no one else other than them and Alix spoke English in the room. Yet, she said nothing and smiled before leaving the men.

As previously decided, when she arrived near the drinks table, she bumped into Alix and, surreptitiously, gave her a

181

dagger before taking a bowl of cider. She went back to Evan and Pierre, who were still in the same corner, and casually talked about the wedding, the weather and the activities they were planning to do the following week. Everything was rehearsed, even the conversation. Evan had a spark in his eye that often contradicted whatever he was saying, and she was finding it very hard to keep a straight face. Evan's power was such that he could make you forget all the unpleasantness of a situation if he wanted to; yet he knew better than to distract his friends on that important day.

Sipping her drink, Vivien kept on examining the room and the people inside, particularly attentive of how they behaved towards each other, the alcohol helping them to loosen their decorum. The Ghost was obviously reigning throughout the room and his family behaved like royalty; yet his wife clearly did not like their daughter. The said daughter made a few lewd comments to the guests and the other son did not drink, trying his hardest to keep away unmarried noble girls from the neighbourhood whilst intently watching Alix. Vivien remembered her friend mentioning that he had helped her; she had read between the lines that there was some sort of romance going on, but it seemed that the flames were still there, perhaps even stronger. She smiled sadly, knowing that regardless of how today went, there was no future for them. She also wondered how come no one else had noticed his eyes, staring at her with such an intensity that Vivien felt her cheeks becoming red.

"What's wrong, dear?" asked Evan, concern both for her and the plan shining in his eyes. It was nothing compared to how the guy looked at Alix, but, at the same time, it was everything for her. Evan did not have to pack all his feelings into one look, as they had tomorrow and all the following days – until one of them got bored of the other.

She shook her head, putting her hand in the crook of his elbow and squeezing. "Nothing."

Pierre looked puzzled; Evan watched her intently, knowing that she was not telling him everything, but he knew and trusted her enough to be sure she would not risk the mission. The moment was interrupted by a very jovial fake Marguerite. "*Bonjour! Vous devez être nos voisins anglais!*" she started enthusiastically. "*Je suis Marguerite de Kerhoët. Je suis ravie de finalement vous rencontrer. J'ai tellement de questions pour vous!*"[17]

Startled by this loud and overly cheerful introduction, the group stayed silent and motionless for a few second before Pierre answered her. Fake Marguerite's interest quickly faded when she realised that the couple could not speak French and that they needed everything to be translated, which took some extra time. Her overactive personality, exacerbated by the alcohol, made her leave the trio quickly – to their relief – to go talk with another group – not as exotic, but civilised enough to speak French.

The party had been going on for some time when, from the corner of her eye, Vivien saw the groom, a stupid, drunken smile on his face, disappear into one of the corridors. Alix glanced at her and nodded. A few minutes after, while checking that no one was paying attention to her, the young

---

17   Hi! You must be our new English neighbours! I am Marguerite de Kerhoët. I am so glad to finally meet you. I have so many questions for you!

bride followed the man, her body tensed. Not long after, she came back, her face white and her hands shaking; she glanced at Vivien and gave her another small nod before going to get another bowl of cider and join a group. She was more relaxed than before, a big and genuine smile on her face, and managed to converse with several people before the party was interrupted. As they had expected, a servant had found the body of Louis, stabbed, in a corridor. Women started to scream and a couple even fainted. Vivien observed Alix, who feigned horror and sadness, and almost started to laugh. Evan took her in his arms, as if comforting her.

"Is it time?"

"Not yet – we need to wait for the guests to leave first, and then we can attack."

Evan looked around. "As soon as those bloody women calm down, people will start to leave. In any case, I think the Kerhoëts'll make us leave soon."

"Damn," swore Vivien.

"I have an idea… Faint and don't wake up."

Offended by such a suggestion, Vivien looked up, shooting him with such an unfriendly glance that Pierre had to hide his laugh behind a fit of coughing. She asserted, "I would never faint."

Evan shook his head and took her in his arms, pretending to comfort her. "I know, but they don't. They think you are a fancy and delicate English lady – what do you think she would have done, learning that someone had been murdered?"

Vivien stayed silent, trying to find a better solution, but came up with none. She sighed. "She would have fainted," she grudgingly answered.

Evan smiled with all his teeth, a malicious flame in his gaze. "Then do it."

"I bloody hate when you are right," she whispered.

"Hurry up, my delicate English flower, they announced the discovery of the body a few minutes ago."

Vivien sighed, stepped back, rolled her eyes and fell on the floor.

Her eyes closed; she felt Evan stopping her fall and people starting to yell around them. Some guests believed that she too had been stabbed and hurriedly left the castle. The others wanted to stay to enjoy the drama, but as soon as the fainting and screaming women went quiet, the Kerhoët family asked them to leave. Vivien waited a few more minutes. She could hear Pierre hurriedly speaking in French until they brought something foul-smelling that made her shoot her eyes open. She pretended to be a bit disoriented, clutching Evan until he whispered in her ear, "It's time."

Evan exchanged a glance with Pierre, who nodded and went out quickly to bring the others. The crew had entered the compound during the marriage ceremony and had been waiting on the ground floor of Marguerite's tower. Weeks ago, Alix had drawn up a plan of the castle that they had all had to memorise. Within minutes, the heavily armed crew was in the room, their pistols aimed at the Kerhoëts.

The Ghost was fuming. "*Que nous voulez-vous?*" As no one answered, he carried on. "*Nous avons de l'argent. Quel est votre prix?*[18]"

Pierre translated that to the crew, who laughed, which

---

18   What do you want from us? We have money. What's your price?

irritated the Ghost further. "*Pourquoi rient-ils ces idiots?*[19]"

"*Parce que tout l'argent du monde n'est pas en mesure de vous sauver…*[20]"

The Kerhoëts turned and faced Alix in disbelief. The young woman smiled, delighted to see them so surprised. She was truly afraid that the Ghost had some doubts about her, but it appeared that his ego was much bigger than they had anticipated. For him, marrying into his family was such a gift that nothing else could compare.

"*Vous nous avez trahi?*[21]" asked the Countess with a mix of fear and disgust.

Alix shook her head. "*Vu que vous prévoyiez de me tuer, je ne pense pas que vous soyez en mesure de me jeter la première pierre.*[22]" Shocked, the Countess opened her mouth and closed it immediately. Alix turned to the Count. "*Peu importe, nous sommes ici pour vous, Fantôme.*[23]"

The Count turned pale; he looked around, as if to find an exit to flee from, but there were none available, as the pirates stood in front of all of them.

"*Nous vous avons cherché très longtemps et, si ce n'était pour votre besoin de jouer au chat et à la souris, nous ne vous aurions jamais trouvé!*[24]" As he looked deeply puzzled, Alix added with

---

19 Why do those idiots laugh?

20 Because all the gold in the world will not save you…

21 You betrayed us?

22 As you planned to kill me, I don't think you are in the position to cast the first stone.

23 Whatever, we are here for you, Ghost.

24 We looked for you for a very long time, and if it wasn't for your need to play cat and mouse, we would have never found you.

a smile, "*Nous somme l'équipage de la* Sirène.[25]" The Count's face became white as he understood that there was no way out for him. "*Non seulement vous avez assassiné notre capitaine, mais notre equipage s'est construit autour des méfaits que vous avez commis; vous êtes un meurtrier et c'est notre désir de revanche qui nous a réunis. Nous allons maintenant vous juger.*[26]"

The Countess and fake Marguerite gasped, the latter very confused by what was happening but too scared to say anything. She clutched her father's arm, looking for comfort, but he pushed her away.

"*Mais pouquoi tuer Louis?*" asked the Countess with a broken and furious voice. "*Il n'a rien fait de tout cela?*[27]"

Alix shrugged. "*Un prêté pour un rendu.*" Seeing the puzzled faces of the Kerhoëts – even Henri, who did not know the story – she answered in a cold voice, "*Il est responsable des souffrances et de la mort de Thérèse, il ne pouvait pas continuer à vivre.*[28]"

The Countess let out a scream. "*Vous l'avez tué! Vous avez tué mon parfait petit garcon?*[29]"

Avoiding Henri's eyes, Alix shrugged again before turning towards the crew. "Ladies and gentlemen of the *Mermaid*, all in favour for the Ghost dying here and now, please say 'aye'."

In one voice, the crew shouted, "Aye."

---

25 We are the crew of the *Mermaid*.
26 Not only did you murder our captain, but our crew has been built from the misdeeds you did; you are a killer and it is our desire for revenge that brought us together. We will now judge you.
27 Then why kill Louis? He did not do anything!
28 Tit-for-tat. He is responsible for the suffering and the death of Thérèse; he could not live.
29 You killed him! You killed my perfect little boy!

Alix nodded and added, "Anyone against his death?"

No one said the expected 'nay'.

Alix turned back to the Count. "*A l'unanimité nous vous condamnons à mort. Nul besoin de dernière volonté, nous n'en avons cure.*[30]" She waited for Pierre to finish up translating her sentence and looked at Vivien. "Captain, the time has come."

Vivien grabbed a pistol and came to Alix, her glance fixed on the Ghost. She was surprised that he looked so scared; one would think that a man who had been skimming the ocean for a decade and fighting other ships would be... more imposing. Their presence had turned the legendary pirate into a man afraid for his life – it was truly pathetic.

"For Michael," she said in a low voice. She could hear the room buzzing with the names of other victims. "For our beloved captain."

She armed the pistol, aimed and shot – straight in between his eyes. Without a sound, he fell on the floor like a rag doll. Fake Marguerite shouted and fainted, whilst the Countess kept her composure, coldly looking at the pirates, contemptuously looking at her fake daughter. Henri remained motionless, as if none of this was happening.

"*Bien, l'équipage va maintenant vous escorter en dehors de l'enceinte du château et nous allons procéder à la seconde phase de notre plan.*[31]"

"*Qu'allez-vous faire?*[32]" asked the Countess with hate in her voice.

---

30 We unanimously condemn you to death. No need for any last wish; we don't care about it.

31 Good, the crew will now lead you outside of the compound and we will proceed with the next phase of the plan.

32 What will you do?

Alix smiled sweetly. "*Vous avez détruits des vies pour votre enrichissement personnel. Nous allons nous assurer que vous n'allez rien retirer des méfaits du Fantôme.*[33]"

The Countess's face became white; she started to shake her head but One-eyed Harry grabbed her arm to bring her outside. Vivien smiled: the Countess had felt barely an emotion when her husband was shot in front of her eyes, but the possibility of losing her money and belongings truly broke her heart. Henri followed them without a word, holding fake Marguerite in his arms. Vivien took control of the situation; she assigned a third of the men to tie up and check on the prisoners, a third to rummage through the castle and find anything of value, and the last third to install gunpowder barrels all over the castle, to ensure that after that day Beg Hastel and its nasty secrets would be no more.

"I'm going to take Marguerite – I told her to be ready."

Vivien nodded and Alix started running into the castle; she felt light. No one would ever replace Thérèse or the captain, but she felt as if they had honoured their memories in ensuring that their tormentors would never hurt anyone else. She arrived at Marguerite's room, out of breath but smiling. She opened the door. "It is time!"

Her friend was a bit startled by that brisk arrival, but she had known it would happen. She stood up and grabbed a heavy bag.

Alix looked at her suspiciously. "You've packed your books, haven't you?"

Marguerite had a sly smile on her face. "You know me well."

---

33 You destroyed lives for your personal gain. We will ensure that none of the Ghost's misdeeds will enrich you.

Alix rolled her eyes. "You know that we would have found new ones for you."

Marguerite shrugged. "I like those ones."

Her friend laughed. "Alright, let's go, we still have a long road ahead of us."

The two girls came down and joined the crew. The Countess and fake Marguerite appeared shocked and they started to shout, but One-eyed Harry, who was nearby, gagged them. Alix mounted a horse and Evan helped Marguerite join her – she was a bit afraid, as she had never been on a horse before, but the girl gripped her friend around the waist. Most of the crew members were on their horses with their loot; the last ones – those in charge of the gunpowder – finally joined them. They had placed and tied up their prisoners at the edge of a wood, far away enough not to be collateral victims of the explosions and fire that were going to destroy the castle.

Vivien looked at her crew. "Let's go."

Alix exchanged a look with Henri before kicking her horse – it felt like yesterday that they had been in a similar position, yet so much had changed in a few years, even in the past few days. She wanted to give him one last kiss, but he was going to stay here with his family and she could not destroy the bond they still shared. For a second, she wished he was coming with her, that they could have a future. But it was too late. Also tied up, he looked sad, but he managed to smile and nod at her, so she knew that he agreed with her actions and that they were not going to see each other again. She smiled back and kicked her horse before he could see the tears trailing from her eyes, hoping that Marguerite was too scared to notice how off she was. She galloped and joined the rest of her crew – her family – on the way to Lorient.

April 1696

The rising sun woke Vivien. Evan was still sleeping soundly, his heavy arm draped over her chest. She tiptoed out of the bed, dressed and joined the workers. Marguerite, who had benefited from Pierre and Alix's teaching, spoke decent enough English now and had decided that she wanted to stay at Hope instead of joining definitively the crew – discovering that she had a nephew probably pushed the balance towards this decision. As she was becoming an official member of the village, its members decided to build her a house, near Maya's, who Peter considered as his mother as much as Alix. Marguerite was very happy in the small village, where her difference was accepted instead of being pointed out and hidden. She felt at ease with the inhabitants, as all of them had suffered great injustices in their lives. Her contribution to the village was helping children and adults learn how to read, write and count. She was glad that her skills, perfected by years of isolation, could be useful in Hope.

Even though untrained in any woodwork, everyone joined and helped to build the house. The work was done in a few days, the last one finishing with a banquet and music. Vivien joined Alix, who was sitting alone, sipping some beer. She had been pretty quiet since the events of January…

"Feeling alright?" asked Vivien.

Alix shrugged. "Yes, I just need time to process things."

"It's been months!" Vivien could not help herself.

Two things had been weighing on Alix's mind – one that she could not mention to her friend. As she was sure she would never meet Henri again, it was pointless to think of or mention him. Yet she could not stop herself and, if she was honest, not being able to talk about him was eating her alive. So she decided to share her other thought. "I know, it's just that we spent so many years tracking the Ghost and now it's done, and I just don't know what to do."

Vivien frowned. "What do you mean?"

"We all became pirates to get vengeance – we had it, but now what? It is dangerous and now that our mission is completed, perhaps we could become… legal?"

"You mean a normal merchant ship?"

Alix laughed. "Not a normal one – I don't think any of us could ever be considered normal!" Vivien elbowed her with a smile. "But yes, we could do legal transactions instead of boarding ships. It would be a new beginning for us and a return to whom the captain was before the death of his son."

Vivien stayed silent for a long time before nodding. "I like that. Except Evan, none of us took on the pirate's life by choice, more by necessity… We'll talk to the others tomorrow." She raised her glass. "To new beginnings."

"To new beginnings," answered her friend before raising a glass with her.